BAD COMPANY

BAD COMPANY

William A. Luckey

GUNSMOKE

This hardback edition 2009
by BBC Audiobooks Ltd
by arrangement with
Golden West Literary Agency

ISBN 978 1 408 46233 1

British Library Cataloguing in Publication Data available.

Printed and bound in Great Britain by
CPI Antony Rowe, Chippenham and Eastbourne

For Saja, Broker, Cheyenne, and all the good ones; and for Roger Hubert.

ONE

HE NEVER WOULD learn. All twenty-two and some years and he still hadn't figured it out. Always opening his yap and letting the words spill loose before he got them sorted out. Goddamn, but he'd put himself in a peck of trouble this time. And there was nothing to do but ride it out.

The rider rubbed at the itch on his neck and absently patted the sweaty seal-brown gelding as the horse rattled on in a ground-covering walk. One long hand wiped at the water collecting under the brim of his battered and dust-paled hat while the odd eyes of the man sparkled with untended thoughts.

It had all come around in a small ranch town, a town carrying a strange name to go with the walleyed folk inhabiting it, sitting on their front steps and worrying over a single peaceable stranger riding through, asking where to stay the night. A town named Carrizozo, a town hard on the ears and the soul of a weary traveler. And that's all Blue Mitchell saw in himself: the weariness of the long miles and the coating of dust he swallowed each day, spanked from his shirt and jeans at night. He was sure enough a harmless traveler, and couldn't figure the folk of this town getting jumpy at his innocent questions.

Blue Mitchell never put much thought to the world outside him, the world printed in the newspapers sold in the small towns. He could read, barely, and he usually had a book

1

stuck in the bags tied to his saddle. He'd ponder over their meanings come nightfall, if he weren't so worn down that he hit the blankets right after hobbling his mount and chewing on something that passed for cooking.

He knew little about himself, only guessed at the length of his six feet and his lean weight when he was bound to buy store clothes. Or when he tried to stuff his once broken toes into new tight boots. Beyond that he had no sense of himself or his presence in the world around him. A lack that often brought with it unwanted and unexpected trouble.

It was his manner that spun the heads around in the town of Carrizozo, that put shaking hands close by shotguns and fancy rifles and old worn Colts. There had been times for Blue when he'd lived in houses like these, close to their neighbors, near enough to smell the morning meal, hear the crying nights. It had worn thin on him so he'd headed out, well mounted on a blooded horse, carrying only the smallest twinge of a memory when he thought on those left behind.

As he hit Carrizozo and saw the hands move to hidden weapons, he worried what he looked like, as if he'd grown a set of horns the past miles, not just the soft yellow beard and extra lines bracketing his mouth, narrowing his eyes. He could not see himself as these town folk saw him.

It was his careless riding of the brown gelding, the hard and arrogant set to him as he sat on the horse, the flow of streaked blond hair over his soiled and collarless shirt. The color of the eyes deep in the hard-boned face had got him his name as a babe and got him in trouble ever since. He could not understand that it was his face and look that kept the world on edge.

If he'd ever seen the ocean, he would have known its brotherhood. Its shifting blue-green waters were mirrored in his eyes; heavy orbs bright in the clarity of surrounding white, taunting and insolent eyes that shielded him from the ordinary prying world. Blue Mitchell, named by a startled father from the brilliant coloring of those eyes, lost early to family and time, ignorant of the rudimentary facts of his beginnings, uncertain even of his age but holding to a given day

2

as his to celebrate. He'd come to manhood early, with an inherent toughness, a sense of the rightness of certain things. And a gift with horses, a knowledge of how to take their nervous energy and create a working ability for others to use. A special skill, caught in the hands and mind of an insolent boy still turning to become a man.

He was nothing more than a bony, long-legged rider born to the hard work and ultimate sadness of a tired land high in the mountains. He'd been hard-used as a child, sold by a great uncle to bring in drinking pennies. He'd learned his letters only by the kindness of a ranch woman, wife of the man his uncle hired him to. Three years of schooling ended with the woman's death in childbirth.

Between the natural gaze of his eyes and his quick-humored tongue Blue stayed constantly in trouble, barely out of reach of certain death. Such as his ride into the sleeping town of Carrizozo and a big-talking, blustering man, who saw Blue and wanted to slam those violent eyes swollen shut. A self-important man who bragged on the ownership of his ranch farther north. Blue had listened, hands spread to show his indifference to the upcoming fight, feet balanced wide for when the fight came to him. He listened to the shouted words and tried to turn them away.

"You son-of-a-bitching glory boy. Ride in here, take what you want, and figure folks'll let you do it in peace. Look at you, you ain't nothin' but a range drifter. Got no worth to you at all, nothing makes you so goddamn special. Hell, you ain't no cowhand, no bronc rider. You just a pretty boy figures the world'll lie down and roll over for you. I got me a horse to my ranch . . ."

The talking made little sense to Blue. He'd said nothing to the man but a polite "Howdy", plus a few comments on the weather and the fair rolling land he'd been riding. The sorry rancher turned crimson-red and let his hand touch the butt of an old pistol. Hell, Blue didn't wear a gun, kept his holstered to the old Mex rig the Señora let him have back near Tucson. He was no hand with a gun. So he let the man talk on till he came to a challenge he understood, and there Blue

3

made his mistake. Opened his mouth and said he'd take the bet, shove it right back down the big man's throat. Give him something to consider other than the smooth feel of the gun hard-held in his hand.

So here he was, pushing the brown gelding to a ranch hidden somewhere in the sloping land around him. He knew he had plenty of company, that men rode in small groups just over the ridges on both sides of him. Men who had listened to the blowing man in the bar and bet on the chance Blue would lose, with the advantage that they knew the mettle of the horse he was to ride. Another mess, and no one to blame but himself. Blue sighed.

A bet on a five-dollar bucking horse, that he would ride it to the ground. A mass of men standing behind the owner of the horse, jeering at Blue, egging the two of them on to make bigger fools of themselves. And here was one of the fools, riding with his unseen escort, headed straight into nothing.

There had been one man out of the crowd Blue'd taken notice of: a big and handsome man, dressed fine in twill pants and a soft tan shirt, silk knotted at his neck, a smooth-pelted Stetson sitting back on his rich brown hair. Couldn't help but pick out the son from the shoving and yelling bettors, most of them eager to take up action on the word of the outlaw's owner. The only man who placed his bets on Blue, and grinned while he did it. Laid out a small pile of shining gold coins and allowed as he thought the drifter could ride down the sainted bay roan.

Blue didn't trust his immediate feelings when he heard the man speak. Purely educated the son was. Spoke fine and clean, with precision to the sounds, with knowledge and money way back in the throat of the words. But the son put his hard money on Blue and swore he'd be to the ranch when the contest went to its conclusion.

Becker Sorrell, that was the name of the man who owned the supposed outlaw and the ranch set deep in the grasslands up ahead. That damned horse must be something special, to pull the number of men from Carrizozo willing to ride the miles to the land behind a town called Vaughn and watch a

4

contest between an unknown ranny and a wicked fire-breathing outlaw son. At least that's the way Becker Sorrell talked of the horse, and the men around him nodded their heads in agreement. All except the big, well-dressed son who put his bets on Blue.

He rode by himself the two days it took from the saloon in Carrizozo to the hanging iron sign at Sorrell's ranch. Blue didn't want the company of the men who rode out of his sight any more than they wanted his. He might have ridden a few miles with the brown-haired man, the one with the purple silk tied around his neck. There was a puzzle in the man, an extra glint to his eyes, a knowing in his pretty smile and clean white teeth. Something Blue didn't understand but had a gut curiousness about. As if past the unholy cleanness of the man there was a grit and an iron that ruled real hard. Blue liked puzzles, found they gave meaning to getting up each morning. And he'd found that meaning lost since he left the Tucson Valley and the ranch set up in the mountains.

Now he was riding to a new challenge: a bay roan outlaw, an unknown bronc said to eat wranglers and spit them out with a wad of hay stuck in their mouths. A real belly-wringing, hightailing wampus cat who could never be rode. So Becker Sorrell had said in his whiskey-soaked spiel, and a good number of men backed up his claims.

Blue kept going over in his head what little he knew, letting it circle and come in gently, land softly, so he could pick through and try to figure things. It was going to be some kind of a day, that Blue Mitchell knew.

Blue camped alone both nights. The first night he laid out a fire and roasted himself a prairie chicken dumb enough to walk past the end of his pistol. He finished the meal on the second. He heard enough loud clicks as his shot echoed on the wide land to scare off an army; his traveling companions must have readied themselves against an attack. They were a nervous bunch. It was the one time traveling a strange land that Blue was comfortable having a fire, roasting his meal

5

real slow to let it have some taste. And he turned in to sleep knowing he was well guarded. Out there, unseen, was a passel of men willing to pistol-whip or gun down anything that walked strange in the night.

It came to him it was like sleeping in a well-guarded jail, a thought that brought Blue awake with a trembling belly. Then he remembered he'd stayed out of jail over a year now, and it was men eager to watch him ride that were guarding him, not a hot-eyed deputy or mustached dog-town law. He lay back down and slept the sleep of the innocent.

That second morning Blue rose quietly and pounded out fresh grounds from a sack of beans. A good night's sleep, a cup of hot coffee to watch the sun come up. These were all the edge a man needed to ride a rank outlaw horse. Sorrell had said his place wasn't far from here. So Blue sat on a rounded stump and let the coffee cool between his hands, let his eyes take in the yellowed sun over the horizon, and thought as little as possible on what was to come.

It was just mid-morning when Blue guided the seal-brown between the high mud-stacked posts that marked Sorrell's place. He wasn't much impressed with the lay of the outfit: corrals that leaned sideways with broken posts, gear spilled and left to sun-rot, a hole in the roof of what could be a bunkhouse. Some fancy bragging on not much. Yet when Sorrell appeared on the sloped floor of the veranda across the house, the man showed himself a proper host.

"You set down, Mr. Mitchell. Slip that-there horse's bit and let him drink clean spring water. Got hot coffee to the stove, biscuits if you wants. Missus baked up a fresh batch."

The man was sly, Blue had to give him that. Acting as if nothing more were happening than putting up a visitor come to the ranch, as if Blue were a welcomed friend. Becker Sorrell was an actor clear enough: putting an extra grin to his slobbered mouth, scratching himself under the heavy weight of his silver buckle, tugging at the back of his pants as if to force them high on his hips. Waiting for an audience that hadn't yet showed up.

"Yessir, you take good care of that brown, tie him to the

6

shade tree if you will. Don't want him bleaching out in this sun, don't want nothing to burn that fine hide of his. You got yourself a mighty good horse there, Mr. Blue Mitchell.''

A woman stepped out on the wide worn boards, came to stand directly behind Mr. Sorrell with a cup steaming in one hand, a plate raising its own hot column of air in the other. Blue nodded to the woman, thanking her with his eyes for the gifts in her hands. She blushed, something Blue knew would happen when he lifted a smile to his face, and she even took a step backwards, as if confused by what her husband had invited to their ranch.

Blue stepped down from the brown gelding, tipped his hat, then made to tie up the horse to the nearest post.

"Ma'am, they smell right good. The biscuits I mean. I thank you.''

She wasn't much of a thing, but she didn't have too many years on her yet. Closer to Blue's age than Sorrell's good forty-odd years and counting. And no sign of a child hanging on her, no thickening to her waist or sagging to the sweet form under her flowered gingham shirtwaist. Blue found himself blushing and he looked again at the biscuits circling the plate, the dark redness of jam mounded in the center. This was a man's wife; he had no cause to be looking her over as if a filly set to breed to the right stud horse. The shame in him coarsened his voice, stuck the words in his throat.

"Ma'am, I do thank you. That plate's a right treat.''

They were both blushing now, faces a matched red and heated from the unexpected thoughts. Blue saw her again, almost felt her touch as he lifted a biscuit out of the circle and dug its warm corner in the piled jam. Straw-blond hair knotted and tucked to the back of her head, soft dark eyes hidden by the tilt of her head, slender fingers scoured rough by chores but holding to a daintiness that couldn't be worked away. She was a sweet filly, no doubt to that. Blue wondered at her marrying Becker Sorrell, wondered at her staying at this rough string ranch with no future.

He shook his head clear of the wandering thoughts, and

7

the husband must have figured he was saying no to a question Blue hadn't heard spoken.

"Good then, Mitchell. You stuff that biscuit where you please and we'll get right to business. I got my hands bringing up the bay roan. Give another hour and all them bettors'll be setting the top rail of the corral. We going to have us quite a sight. Yessir, quite a sight."

Blue looked hard at the man then and didn't like the growing width to his smile or the hands wiped together, over and over, as if touching and retouching a pile of money or the soft gleaming coat of the seal-brown horse.

"Hitty, you take that coffee and biscuits back inside. Mister Blue Mitchell's done with your cooking. He got other things on his mind now, men's things. Get."

Hitty? Hell of a name for such a pretty thing. Blue'd bet himself it was a shortening of some fancy name the damn fool Sorrell couldn't say or didn't like. Something more in keeping with the shifting of the long skirt as her backside disappeared past the black hole of the doorway and was gone. All that was left of the woman was a slightly tangy hint of berry jam and a powdered taste of dry biscuit in Blue's mouth. Blue laughed at himself then, for letting his attention get so far off the mark. He looked at his host, suddenly suspecting the man was far more clever than he would have guessed. The thought of using a wife to distract a man, lose him his edge, put a set to Blue's stomach and a hardness back in his mind.

The yard had started to fill up, horses tied in companionable bunches to sagging posts and stripped-bark trees. Tails slapped and blew against drifting flies, hooves stamped and bits rattled as the horses shifted position to find a meager share of comfort as they dozed in the sun.

The pretty man with the purple silk rag tied to his neck hadn't come in yet. He'd been mounted on a smooth-limbed gray, a horse tall enough and rugged enough to hold the man's considerable bulk. There had been silver strapped to the gray's rigging, silver worked in the fancy curb that hung from the braided slip-ear bridle. The boots were plain, that much Blue remembered, plain enough to belong to a working cowhand.

Blue shaded his eyes and looked to the corral, wondering about the outlaw roan. Then Sorrell's grating voice interrupted him.

"By god, Teller made it. Guess it's on his way, come to think of it. Right on the trail to that land he claims is a ranch north of here. So Teller's going to follow through his bragging on you, Mr. Mitchell, and sit right here and pay out good money to back his words. You best be ready to speak up to him why you lost the ride, sonny. He got a pile of money on you."

So, the pretty-faced man's name was Teller. Teller what, or what Teller? Spoke all right, either way. Blue didn't much care. But he did want to know why this one man, out of a bunch of hard-riding, short-spitting rannies, would back a stranger's bragging with a pile of gold coin and a quick grin. As if he knew something on Blue the others missed, as if he saw what Becker Sorrell and his *compadres* went past. Blue didn't like it, the feeling a man knew him too quickly.

But he did know he could ride the bay roan. There wasn't a horse he couldn't ride. Maybe one or two, but not many. He'd made the brag all right, and now he had to ride it out. He could ride anything, given his own time, his own way. But this, a circle of hollering men and gold-matched bets, this wasn't his way of riding any man's horse.

Blue shook his head again, felt the strands of tangled hair slap his shirt, stick to the sweated crease of his neck. He lifted his shapeless hat and wiped at the heavy mane, swept it back from the hooded blue of his eyes, and jammed the hat back down. Best keep his sight clear, his head free. It was going to be one hell of a ride.

A weight settled down next to him on the middle step of Sorrell's veranda stairs. A good deal of weight, from the wood's groaning, and Blue glanced sideways without really turning his head. Didn't want to have his neighbor think he was nosy. Just wanted to know who would choose to sit next to him and stare out to the dusty yard, filling with more men dismounting and tying their horses, slapping their friends on the back, talking in excited voices about the bay roan and the big-mouthed kid.

Of course, it was the pretty-faced man, Teller something. With the smooth silver hat shoved back on the dark hair, the light shining in the silk of his hazel eyes. Had a real friendly grin to the corners of his mouth, and Blue found himself echoing the sight, felt the pull of his lips as he returned the easy gesture. The man didn't stare, but looked down at his own hands clasped between his knees and let his voice work its considerable magic.

"Mitchell, is it? Blue Mitchell? You got yourself quite an audience this morning for your intended activity. I will say, Sorrell's roan is quite the bucker, a regular outlaw. But then, my friend, you are an outlaw of your own."

Blue stiffened at what could have been an insult, but the man shifted direction faster than the seal-brown gelding and caught Blue off guard.

"I hope my betting on you hasn't made you nervous. I believe, from my last tally, that I have close to five hundred dollars in coin riding on you, so to speak. I surely hope that doesn't make you nervous, Mr. Blue Mitchell."

The man was playing with him, telling him to relax and then tallying up the money as if he had already gone belly-up on the roan. Putting the spur to his ribs before Blue even got to see the so-called outlaw. The man was playing his game with Blue as the pawn, and Blue didn't take kindly to the implication.

"Teller, it's your money. And my ride. You bet how you like. I know what I can do."

He judged his refusal to be baited put a glint in the pretty man's eyes. But there was a bellowing from the corral behind a barn and a man's yelling that joined it, with some high cowboy hooraying to make up the chorus. They must of got in the roan; it was time.

Before Blue stood his full height, he felt the boards shift and sag under his feet as Teller Something came up beside

10

him. He glanced at the big man's face, saw nothing but innocent pleasure in the quick hazel eyes, and knew an answering pleasure in his own mind. A clean ride, a game of high stakes, a challenge to be met and taken. Blue would come back to this man after the ride's end. After he rode the bay roan.

If he rode the bay roan.

TWO

THE HORSE DIDN'T look like much, and that worried Blue. Not rough and pig-eyed, not smooth and well muscled and hot; just a smallish roan gelding with faded black points, a shaggy mane, and a burr-matted tail, cattails hanging to his hocks. No wild killer light in the dark eye, no laid-back long ears or high-boned Roman nose. A tough, sturdy cow horse with some age, splints on both front legs, hooves splayed wide and chipped, back and sides saddle-galled and dotted with dollar-sized white spots.

The signs were there: that the horse was barefoot in this flint-hard ground, that sores on its back went untreated, that the mane and forelock were tangled to the point of slapping the horse, the tail a disaster of braided neglect. No one wanted to handle this horse any more than necessary, yet pride would not let the owner turn it loose or kill it for hoof and hide.

At a signal from Becker Sorrell two men slipped up on either side of the gelding and cast small loops over the high arched head. The roan barely shied at the quick movements, and stood to be saddled with only an occasional sideways kick to remind the men of his well-deserved reputation. As if the horse knew, the small head twisted, the eyes circled the yard until they pinpointed Blue and remained fixed on him. The ears pricked, the nostrils flared wide to take in the scent of the challenger.

Blue walked alone to the corral; the men scrambled on

either side of him, anxious to have a good perch on the high-railed wall. They held a space for him at the open gate that led him directly to the outlaw roan. Blue knew the gate closed behind him but he didn't take his eyes from the roan, nor did he acknowledge the catcalls and hollers of the men hanging from the fence.

The roan barely twitched when the ground-men removed their ropes and stepped back quickly, out of range of the chipped hind feet. The matted tail switched back and forth on the sweated flanks, and the soft thumping sound was un-nerving. Blue went to the horse's head and threaded his left hand in the cheek piece of the hard leather halter. He steadied the roan head back to the wet shoulder, looked deeply into the flecked eye, and murmured a curse to himself. He ran an expert hand over the saddle rigging, testing its security on the humped back. Then he shifted his weight onto the balls of his feet, tugged his hat down hard on his own matted hair, and was ready.

Sorrell's voice broke into his thoughts, sent a shudder through him that was echoed in the roan's twitching skin.

"Mitchell, you ride that horse to a standstill. Till he won't buck no more. Or the brown is mine."

That was the deal, that was the big bet. There was no discussion needed, no further speaking of the words. But their sound caught in the walled pen was enough to unbal-ance Blue, to let the roan take his head and pull an extra inch of rein. Blue rewound the rope in his hand, took a deep breath, jabbed his foot in the iron stirrup, and eased onto the bay roan's humped back.

The outlaw was a master at this game; he let Blue set him for a second, let Blue find his off stirrup, let him tug at his hat again, wind the rope in slippery fingers, take another deep breath.

It was at the end of the breath, when Blue was beginning to wonder, that the bay roan bogged his head and bellowed once, loud enough to wake the dead in Texas, and went straight up, twisting sideways, coming down headed in the other direction. Blue had a sense of flying, saw the specked

13

shoulders swing in front of him, and felt the head swivel at the end of the loosened rope. He swayed with the roan's effort, guessed at the next high leap, and drove spurs along the wide sprung ribs.

The bay quit bellowing, took three dancing leaps off his hind legs, and slammed sideways into the railed fence. A sitter on the top row tumbled back and fell, knocking himself out. No one noticed. Blue drove in the right spur, impaled his boot in the roan's ribs, heard the horse scream an answer as he reared to the top of his height, balancing on one hind hoof, threatening, teasing, testing Blue.

Blue leaned forward and cuffed his free hand over the roan's right eye, insulting the horse with the casual slapping. The bay roan dropped to his knees, and Blue went over the high metal horn which caught on his belt. When the roan came back up, Blue was held forward and helpless. The bay roan knew it, felt the awkward balance; spun wildly to the left, dropped a shoulder, and bucked in a high forward leap. Blue lost his near stirrup, grabbed for the sliding rope, and took a gut-slamming blow from the horn that almost tore him in half.

The horn slipped free and Blue jammed himself into the rhythm of the roan, reached his spurred boots across the lathered shoulders, and punished the angry horse until it lost direction and slammed again into the corral fence and went down hard, skidding on his side.

Blue rolled from the falling body, rolled into the wide-braced post and felt blood run quick through his mouth from the blow along his jaw. He pushed up from the post, staggered on wobbling knees, turned on a high boot heel, and lunged for the roan, catching the narrow horn as the horse struggled to his feet. Blue used the roan's confusion to find the saddle again and jam his feet hard against the ridge of the iron stirrups.

The roan needed no goading; high, wide, and hard the animal leaped. Ears lashed back, tail wringing in awful time to the great bucks, the roan covered the wide corral and spun in midair, jarred to the distant ground on braced front legs,

14

squatted and leaped, spun out again, dropped a shoulder, and shied a soaking head away from the unraveled rope. Blue stayed with the horse, no longer conscious of anything but the insensate motion, the spinning cloud of earth, the smell and the sound of the raging horse between his legs.

He didn't know of the red lines that came from his clenched mouth or streaked from his nose, or those that trickled from his ears to stain his shirt back and collar band. He didn't know of the blood that flowed from the roweled path of his spurs, or the specked foam that flew from the roan's widened nostrils and covered the raging spectators. He couldn't hear their roaring, couldn't see their flailing arms, their faces white under shoved-back hats.

It was Blue and the spinning horse, only Blue and the embattled roan. The roan went down again, slower this time, to groan and lie on his side, heaving in great gasps of air, eyes shut, head skinned raw by the graveled dirt and the dragged line to Blue's hand. Blue knelt by the horse, loosened the line, tried to stand by himself until the bay roan came to his knees like a cow and stayed there, sides laboring, eyes still wild, breath a red foam circling the drawn mouth. The raucous audience was silent; even Becker Sorrell's big mouth was open and wordless.

The roan climbed to wobbly legs, planted the chipped black hooves wide apart, and blew an expanded snort that covered the rider standing too close to him. Then the roan felt something that had never been done to him before: A hand, a man's hand, went over his head softly, touched his ears and stroked them, came down to the flat plane of his jowl and dared to cup the distended muzzle.

The bay roan didn't take to the familiarity; the horse widened long teeth and clamped down on the offending arm above the wrist, then tried to swing a hind leg into kicking range. The audience above horse and rider roared; the roan pulled back on the mouthful of flesh, spat out the terrible taste, swung his quarters and let out a powerful kick.

Blue felt the teeth shred his arm, then the vise let go and he was turned and doubled by the kick. He hit the corral fence, hung there a moment, and watched the blood run from his mangled arm to his shoulder and ribs. Bright red, too near his eyes. He was tired, numbed, bewildered by the streaks in the faded cloth of his shirt. His back hurt near the last rib and over his kidneys. He couldn't remember what was happening; there were words shouted at him, voices that demanded something. Then he raised his head and saw the grinning face of the bay roan.

Blue didn't listen. The war between himself and the horse wasn't done yet. He pushed away from the fence, tearing at grabbing white hands that tried to hold him still. He stood unaided, swaying gently. Then he walked to the bay roan, whose own head hung inches above the stirred ground, whose sides were slowing in their terrible reach for air. The long tail hung to the ground, the black-tipped ears were loose, as the bay's head came up and a red-rimmed eye examined Blue. The horse took one step away from the man, and Blue knew the battle wasn't finished. Not till he rode the son to a standstill, and the bastard was moving, without him as the rider. It wasn't over yet.

He pulled the halter, dragged himself closer to the bay's ribs, and found himself on the wrong side, the off side, the side Eastern ladies who didn't know a damn and painted Indians with eagle feathers and naked asses used to get on a bronc. The wrong side, dammit. But he was too tired to make the long journey around the bulk of the swaying red horse. He jammed a foot to a stirrup and checked again, so he wouldn't be facing tail-end once he got the strength to mount.

The bay's head came around sideways, a questioning look to the eye. Blue didn't bother to head the horse, to draw his face to his shoulder. Took more than enough effort to find the right foot and reach it that high to the jiggling iron stirrup. Goddamn, he was tired, and there was something sticky on his face, something gumming up his throat and making breathing a chore. There was something wrong low down on his back, something he didn't remember happening. He shook his head and regretted the motion.

Then he eyed the bay roan, who looked straight at Blue

16

and sighed deeply. It weren't over yet. The long burred tail slapped gently on the drying sides. Blue tugged down his hat.

He was in the saddle; the bay roan staggered two steps and leaned on the corral fence. Blue took a breath and spat to the side, refusing to see the streaks of red in the dusty glob. He touched the horse with his heels, careful to keep the punishing spurs away from the tender, raw sides. The horse groaned, an echo of the sound burying itself inside Blue, and took an uneasy step from the supporting fence. Then two more strides, urged on by the demon sitting the high-swelled leather cinched to his middle. There was an indignity to the process of being ridden that the bay roan outlaw resented. He remembered, deep in his mind, that this had been tried before and he hadn't liked it then.

So the exhausted horse put his head down, jerked on the line held in loose fingers, and was free of the hated rider's guidance. He tried a buck, found enough energy to come six inches off the ground in a crow hop, and then tried for another. There was a strangled sound from the man on top of him, and odd, nervous laughter from the crowd on the fence rails above him.

The horse squatted, lashed his tail, wagged his head, and flattened his ears. Threats, to make the rider take notice. But the man astride the roan did little more than touch the animal on the white-salted shoulder and use clenched knees and shaking thighs to urge him to move forward. The roan had to move from the pressure, to step forward in one stride and then another, and a universal sigh went along the rails as the horse lifted for a moment into a jarred trot, then halted in response to the line pulled on his nose. And stood still.

"You did it, Mitchell. Never thought I would see the day. . . . Man, that was something."

Blue dismounted to hands reaching for him. He saw blurred faces in front of him, felt taps on his shoulder and back, congratulations spoken in awed and muted tones. The incessant sounds bothered him, the touching tightened his stomach, boiled in his face, until the men stepped back from the wild

17

rider with the raging eyes and pale and bloodied face. They didn't understand, but they knew enough to give him room.

"Mitchell. Blue. Come here, man, set down before you fall."

That was a voice he recognized, a sound he trusted for some goddamn reason. Blue angled toward the noise, uncertain of the pictures his eyes gave him. Wavy lines, white spots that shifted and spun around, shadows that disappeared before he could figure their form. One shadow came up larger than the others, joined by another, smaller form, carrying something. Blue felt as if these two were safe and he could believe in them.

He almost made it, but a pebble the size of a boulder rose up in front of him and caught his toe, dragged him down by its sheer immense size. Blue tumbled forward, unable to put out his hands to break the long fall. Someone caught him with strong arms that held him from the slanting earth, that lifted him back on wobbling feet and led him to a graduated series of pieces of wood, where he thought to sit down and misjudged, had to rest against those arms again before he felt the comforting hardness of the planks beneath his tender butt. There was a shakiness in his hands and legs, an utter weariness behind his eyes.

"Mr. Blue Mitchell, you are one hell of a rider. That was something. Something to see. You could have killed that bronc, but you rode him quiet around that pen as if it were a Sunday outing in the park. That was a ride."

It was the voice Blue thought he might have liked, once, some time back. Liked enough to open his eyes to the words and look into the face of their speaker. He was right. It was that Teller, the one who had either a first or a last name but didn't say which. The one with the fancy purple silk tied to his neck and the silvered hat shoved back on his fine head. Blue purely admired the color of that silk neck rag.

The hazel eyes were smiling at him, and the strong hands that had grabbed him now offered something. A shiny silver bottle with its top peeled off. The man had a gift for silver: silver hat, silver bottle, saddle stamped with shining

18

silver. Silver voice and smile. Now Blue remembered. He couldn't pass up the fine smell coming from that silver bottle held close to his nose, a smell of quality, a smell of good Kentucky sipping whiskey.

The first taste scalded his gums, set them on fire, and Blue instinctively rinsed the liquid around his mouth and spat to the side. Almost apologized for the misuse of the fine liquor, but he looked to the hazel eyes and saw an understanding in them. So he nodded to the bottle, ready for a second try. This one stayed easier in his mouth, as if the burned flesh had released all its fire.

It was a pleasure to reach out with both hands, even though he frowned at their shaking, take the silver bottle from the smiling man and lift it to his mouth, tilt his head back and swallow the next three swallows like they was mother's milk. Nothing ever tasted so good, not even from dear old mother herself.

Blue sat a moment longer to let the whiskey flow through him, numb him completely. Then he tried poking and prodding at his body, curious about the settling pains. He had himself a new horse now, and a piece of that gold to the amount of fifty dollars. About what the señor had promised for the delivery of a special mare and foal to that high ranch in the prickly country southwest of where he was now. Blue shook himself; memories came hard over him, swallowed him whole. He needed to think more on the horse he would choose, a place where he could bed the night to sleep off the sore bones and scraped skin. He spat again, this time not wasting the whiskey, and scrubbed a hand fiercely over his face, wincing from the various sores he disturbed. The next few hours looked to be a plain bore.

Teller Bartlett John watched the roughened man seated beside him and marveled at the constitution that held the man upright. The beating he had taken from the roan should have had him safely tucked in a white hospital bed with attendants hovering around him, doctors whispering in great conferences to the side.

It was one of the mysteries of the West to Teller John that the beatings and shootings and stabbings and general miseries that would lay out a man in the great city of Boston and its environs were ignored out here past the Mississippi River and beyond. It took almost a mortal blow to lay out a man for any length of time.

And here was a fine example: It was as if, because the man could not see the damage, he could not feel its effects. Or the horse, for that matter. The roan was unbridled and stripped of its saddle. Blood was caked on the lathered sides, and salt had dried to white crusted streaks down all four legs, yet the horse stood to a pile of wispy hay and chewed reflectively as if nothing had happened in the past hour. As if the rider seated on the bottom slab of the tilted steps had not beaten and spurred and otherwise brutalized it into fighting to the end, and losing. There was a calm acceptance to the horse that bewildered Teller John, almost to the exclusion of the man beside him.

He swung his thoughts back to Mitchell with an effort. The man couldn't stay here, not on Sorrell's place, after he'd rode the man's bragged outlaw into abject submission. Teller John knew Sorrell well enough to doubt the man's careful hospitality. And Mitchell couldn't be left alone, not from the looks of him, no matter how tough these cowboys said they were.

Even the man's outrageous eyes were blood-streaked, from the tiny vessels inside that had burst with the ride's wild pressure. Blood caked and spotted the long face, was dried to brown lines on the bony hands and across the swollen and ridged knuckles. Teller had seen the contents of the first spit and had shuddered at what it told him. He'd been a medical student at Harvard, considered a most promising student of the medical profession, until a small matter had gotten out of hand and Teller John had come west for his family's health.

Even more than the dried blood and the fevered eyes, it was the final kick of that demonic horse that worried Teller. He'd heard its force, seen it land in the small of Mitchell's back. He would bet, if the man had the energy to relieve himself, there would be traces of blood along with the urine.

The loose boards of the veranda rattled, and Teller guessed it was the woman who'd come to the top step. He guessed she would have a concerned frown on her face, would have those small white teeth caught on her lower lip, her eyes filled with Mitchell's pain. She would be holding a pan of warm water, and there would be bandages under her arm, a can of that terrible-stinking black salve they used on everything out here: cattle, horses, pigs, people. Teller had to admit the stuff seemed to work.

Teller John looked up and saw the pretty face, watched as Mrs. Sorrell sat down near the battered rider. The man smiled at her—he couldn't help but smile at her prettiness—and there was red gummed between his teeth, ragged skin hanging from his lower lip. Hitty Sorrell bent over the pan and rinsed out a cloth, touched it to the chewed mouth, and wiped ever so gently.

Both men were entranced by Mrs. Sorrell; they could see the loosened button at the base of her throat and could imagine the flesh that rose under the tight-checked blouse and folded in again at her banded skirt, demurely covered with a stained apron. Blue shut his eyes; Teller swallowed heavily. The woman coughed discreetly and picked up the red-stained cloth, wrung it out carefully and laid it over her arm, then walked away from the two men.

They sat in silence for some time, both caught in the embarrassment of the moment. Blue shifted his head slightly, felt a pull of muscle across his back. He could see Teller John out of the corner of his eye. The man's face was pale and set and his heavy mouth chewed carefully, as if there were something caught in his teeth that needed removal.

There was a sudden clattering noise; Blue saw a slender hand place a tin bowl, with clean water tipping over the rim, on the floorboards beside him. The can of black salve smelled thick and raw, the cloths were folded precisely, the words spoken clearly.

"Mister, I think it best you do your own tending. Mr. John here can help you. I have other work to do."

21

THREE

"MITCHELL, YOU SURE could do with a haircut, along
with a few days of rest and repair. Good lord, man, you are
a bloody mess."

Blue stiffened; there was laughter behind Teller John's
words, laughter that dug into Blue's dignity. He stared at
Teller John, and the man stared back at him. Inches from
each other, there was a long pause of motionless silence,
then Blue fought a grin, saw it mirrored in John's heavy face,
and finally both men laughed.

Sorrell's yard was almost cleared of men. Only two horses
waited tied under a tree, along with Blue's fine gelding and
Teller John's rugged gray. Blue hadn't gotten to picking out
his horse yet, hadn't found the energy to rise from the roughened board seat. Teller John had been working on him for a
good half hour and Blue was surprised with the gentleness
in the man's thick hands, as if there were a taught skill in
those wide fingers. He shied from thinking on Mrs. Sorrell
and her reasons for leaving Teller to do the healing work. It
was done, and Blue was ashamed.

Blue came back to watching John, and the words still
caught him by surprise:

"Mitchell. Blue. That's an odd name, although I can see
what possessed your parents. . . . Blue Mitchell, I would
offer you a ride to my ranch. A chance to rest up a bit, think
on what you do next. This isn't an offer out of pure kindness,

22

but from the fact of you winning me a good deal of money today. And a pair of horses to boot. So I will offer you a stay at my ranch, a portion of the winnings if you wish."

Blue didn't think much before he told Teller John yes, he'd ride out with him. Wherever home was. And it wasn't kindness on his part either to take the invite; some poking around with his thumb had found sore spots across his back, and his tongue wiggled a few loosened teeth. His arm ached inside the tightly packed bandage, and Blue didn't want to think on the colors he'd become in a few days or the ache of bruised muscle and bone. It was pure selfishness led him to accept Teller John's invitation.

He listened to Teller John with half a mind, the words doubling their sound from the pounding of his tired head.

"There is another reason for my asking you to ride out with me. Blue . . . ah, if I may use your given name . . . I have purchased the rights to a ranch in the middle of some beautiful country north of here. Miles of grassland, belly-high to a good horse. Miles of it."

John's voice trailed off and Blue stopped listening, focused on the throbbing in his arm, the companion complaint in his back. Good goddamn. Then John started up again, his tone warming with the anger of his words.

"But to my shame, the land is being brutalized. By squatters. Men who are loose-herding too many animals, who graze the land until the roots turn up and die, shrivel from their casual destruction, while these men drive their herds farther on for more plundering. They don't care about the land, only the few extra pounds of tallow they might put on their cattle free of charge.

"I have bought a thousand acres, with a ranch house of sorts, and the rights to water. A most precious resource up on the mesa. And I have leased the remaining grazing rights. Now I must convince these squatters that they are trespassing on my land."

Teller John paused then, and Blue found he was listening to the words and could guess at what was coming. He was no gun hand, no straw boss willing to oversee the death of his men and the death of the squatters. Death always came when men fought over cattle and land. Blue didn't want to hear the rest of the story Teller John was outlining. He knew its bitter conclusion.

But Teller John beat Blue to the next words.

"Mitchell, you look at me as if you already know what I am about to ask of you. But please, please listen. I know few men in this land who have shown your courage, or your common sense. I am not asking you to kill; I can hire a gunman as quick as snapping my fingers. What I would like from you is, ah . . . How can I explain this?

"Mitchell, you have shown me something lacking in most men. A sense of honor, and humor. And good judgment. That is all I am asking of you. Do you understand?"

There was a breathing space while Blue sucked in air and began to understand. He didn't like what was coming, so he grabbed more room and spoke first.

"Mr. John, you don't know what you're aiming at, leastways not out here. Could be things are done differently back where you come from.

"You don't ask for friendship. Ain't done that way. And I ain't never had a friend, never such as you talk about. You're looking for a range boss, believe me. Hire a man knows the land, who's worked for other men mosta his time. Offer him a share in your land, then you'll have your friend and your good advice too.

"Me, I'm a horse-breaker, a drifter. Nothing more to me than that."

An unexpected bout of good sense kept John from making a bigger mistake than he already had; kept him from offering money after first trying friendship. This was one time he kept his mouth clamped down and his hand out of his pocket. He knew that Blue Mitchell would stand up and walk away from any such gesture now.

"Blue. Forget what I said. I'm headed out to the ranch. You're still invited along. Got me a fine team of matched blacks and a new spring wagon. It won't be much better than setting a horse, but there's some comfort to the padded seat

24

and leafed springs. Had the wagon made in Denver, and Sorrell's been readying the team for me. Now, because of your ride, I got the team and their training free.

"Sort of planning on there being a Mrs. Teller John one day, and I want to be ready when she comes along. It might turn out to be a courting buggy, you never can tell."

The man was using the sound of his words to coat over the rough spot of his asking and Blue's refusing. Blue knew that much, and he approved. So he grinned at Teller John and put out his hand.

"Sounds 'bout right to me, Mr. John."

There was no more possibility that Blue could stay to the Sorrell place, not with the brown-eyed filly peeking out behind a curtained window and the angry man who was her husband standing straddle-legged in the middle of the yard.

It had been no problem when Blue asked for his coin, although Sorrell did try to hand him a piece of the paper money. But Blue would have none of it, and Sorrell grinned then and put a hand to his pocket and found a rubbed and shiny coin.

The fuss came when Blue chose his horse. Although the deal had been clear right at the beginning, with enough of the town as witnesses, Blue was caught off guard when Sorrell tried to back out. Any horse to the ranch, he'd said, any horse at all.

Blue chose a clean-limbed bay gelding, coming six years, steady to a rope, willing to reach out and snuff Blue's hand when he first caught up the horse. He'd found the gelding in the back, in with a bunch of half-wild two-year-olds. Stained with sweat marks, coated in rolled mud, but still high-headed and proud.

Sorrell blustered some, then backed up on his words and said, "Any other horse but this one: had him a bad tendon, would come up lame on you." Blue didn't listen but put his hand to the horse's withers and scratched the tender place that made the bay stretch his neck and wiggle his lip. Blue had seen the slight thickness on the tendon, felt the smallest

25

of heat. Time would heal that just as it would heal Blue. And the gelding was worth the time.

Blue knew that for certain when Becker Sorrell got ugly, let his hand touch the tip of the pistol worn on a scarred belt. The man's loose mouth flapped around some heavy words about Blue's parentage and his good sense, until Blue lost the good humor that had come to him with finding the bay. He stood braced in front of the mealy-mouthed bastard who was backing out of a fair bet.

There was a moment when trouble could have started, until the remaining two men mounted their horses and rode over to stand above Becker Sorrell. Their presence was enough to turn the scum back into the semblance of an honest man, while Blue picked up the line to the bay and walked slowly out of range of the blistering words. Sorrell was caught now, reminded of the bet by the two neighbors setting on their broncs. There would be no gunplay over a bay gelding and the wild-eyed rider who was taking the animal as free payment.

It was finally the sour-faced bastard Becker Sorrell who shoved Blue into climbing the wheel of the fancy red-striped rig belonging to Teller John and settling to the softness of the plump canvas cushions. He'd never ridden in such a fine rig, never needed to before. Once the sharpness of the conflict with Sorrell fell away Blue began to feel the bruises and the bangings of his argument with the bay roan. Each move of the black team put an ache in him he didn't want to own. John must have heard the small groan that got past Blue's bitten lips, for his hands suddenly tightened on the reins. But for once the man had the sense to keep his mouth quiet, and only slowed the pair to a walk from their high-stepping, showy trot. To give the team a breather, Teller John said, but it was to ease up on the rigidness of Blue's back, the knot swelling behind his red-burned eyes, the funny white dots swimming past his sight. Blue was grateful for the man's good sense and let the warmth of the slow day soothe his bones.

* * *

26

So Blue came into the high mesa country that Teller John claimed was his laid out flat in the back of a red-striped, fancy wagon. Two horses trotted behind the rig and a third, a hard-muscled gray, moved along near the driver. A scrolled Sharps lay across John's lap and a box of shells rested between his feet. There was a pistol snug inside a carved holster tied to his waist, and a short-range shotgun rested on the empty cushion beside him.

John paid little attention to the man sleeping in the wagon bed. Worn down by the morning's work, that was all. Fevered some from the blow across his back, the torn bite on his forearm. Teller had medicines to his half-raised house that would clean and disinfect the arm, and a potion to give him a good night's sleep, perhaps well into the next day. He wasn't worried about Blue Mitchell now. But he was worried about the close bunches of lank cattle tearing into his grass, the riders seen occasionally on the horizon. His hand strayed to the comfort of the shotgun's inlaid stock.

Teller knew he had bought up more than he'd paid for, and he knew he was damned if he gave in to this fight. He glanced back one more time at the man sleeping noisily in the wagon and had a rare twinge of conscience. From what he'd seen of Blue Mitchell, he would take his hospitality and then return the gesture by joining the fight. Teller was counting on Blue's dependability in this facet of western behavior. No man was beholden to another, no man left a debt unpaid.

Blue Mitchell would soon be caught up in Teller's debt. Teller knew himself, knew his weakness. He would let the man take up his cause, and have only a mild regret if and when the man failed. It was an old pattern. His own father, his mother and two sisters, a brother, all had been touched and burned by his dabbling in illicit drugs at the teaching hospital. Teller had not been jailed or charged, and he'd fled from the scorn.

Now he was repeating the pattern, letting others fight for him. Letting others bear the burdens he should assume. Using the strengths of other men, buying their compliance with a strong smile and a silver bottle of bonded whiskey. A few

27

carefully placed words. There was a sense of regret in Teller, and vague disappointment, as he saw the undefeated rider's features rise before him. They were clear enough in the afternoon sunlight, as if the man were talking to him, smiling at him from that odd bony face, watching with those wonderful and frightening ocean-blue eyes. The blue off the island of Nantucket on a sun-warmed winter's day.

Disappointment. Regret. Unusual feelings for Teller, toward a man he barely knew. A rootless drifter, still almost a boy, face covered in soft sprigs of beard, blond hair tangled and pretty as a farm girl's. Disappointment at the thought that his betrayal of a man who meant nothing to him might grow a knot of regret inside him he hadn't felt for his austere father and tight-faced mother.

Teller John slapped the blacks, angry at the blend of unwanted emotions derailing his careful plans. He let the horses run a long distance across the mesa. His mesa. Goddamn it, *his* mesa.

He slowed the horses to a walk as they came to the rude cabin built that summer for a pretty girl. The daughter of his new enemy. Teller smiled to himself as he saw the flash of color, the quick lift and drop of a slender hand, that would be Miss Thomas Ann Whitlow, curious as to who was driving across the mesa.

Once past the small cabin, he touched the horses to a quicker pace. Feelings of regret came back to him again, cutting through his belly. That damned disappointment. As if those remarkable blue eyes under their bony ridged brows had already sat in judgment on him and found the lack most others missed, the hole glossed over by gracious manners and a thick wallet. A silver stream of words. Even when he lied Teller John could look straight on a man and never blink or flinch. It was one of his multitude of talents.

He thought again on Blue Mitchell and shook his head, completely angry at himself for the treacherous invading thoughts. He needed the man's rough manner, his quick temper and fast and agile mind. Nothing more than that. The words of friendship almost spoken earlier had been some of

28

Teller's ready lies, no truth behind their unfinished sentiments. There was no changing the spots of a yellow-backed
leopard. Teller had read that somewhere and knew it for truth.

FOUR

Tom Whitlow watched his daughter move between the crude bowl scooped out of a storm-blown pine knot and the waiting bucket of water. Watched her work to clean up after the hands had mangled her fine-cooked meal, then tried to stick out their feet and roll and light a smoke. His child took offense then and swiped at the lot of them with the black-greased fry pan. Tom Whitlow had laughed, even though it wasn't good politics, as he watched the wild-haired rannies run from his child, his Thomas Ann. As if his daughter were the wife of the devil himself.

He'd tried to make things comfortable for his Annie. He'd gotten the crude log cabin built, and even gone to the trouble of putting up a wall for a private room all her own. He'd worked over the small corner of the room, layering ends of rough lumber to build Annie a shelf for her precious treasures. He'd never known a woman, a girl really, to cradle things as did his Thomas Ann. Annie, she wanted to be called, or sometimes, when she was feeling fancy, Anna. As if to make up for the mistake of having a man's first name.

Tom Whitlow refused to think on the why of his child's name. It had been his woman's choice, and she was dead. So it was Thomas Ann Whitlow, and there was nothing he would say on the matter.

The bent and tired old man looked around, trying to see the cabin's interior from Annie's view. It was a rough affair by any standards, but then he knew they wouldn't be here come winter. The men who'd signed on to work for him and his partner had taken apart an old cabin and rebuilt it for the girl. A sagging and abandoned cabin that got pulled down, the logs dragged to where Annie said she wanted to look out a window. Tom didn't see what was special about that particular place, just more miles of grass dotted with piñon and some juniper. But Annie wanted her home built in the juniper, so the boys were careful not to damage the trees while they dragged in the logs and built the cabin to her whims.

There were three of the men working for Tom Whitlow, and five more who called Emmett Blaisdel their boss. In a way the cabin's building had been a blessing: It had given these hardcases something to do before the cattle cleaned out the small meadow. The men purely loved to work for Miss Annie, in the hopes she would smile for them. Or make a fresh pan of biscuits and a dried-apple pie. All except Emmett Blaisdel; he hadn't known Whitlow had a child, and had objected violently when he found out the girl would be joining them on the mesa. Tom Whitlow had stayed firm to his decision, and for once Emmett backed down.

"Emmett, you know I can't just up and leave the girl. I'm all she's got. You watch, she'll cook for the men and they'll be willing to give their life for her. She's a good girl, and a tough one. And I ain't leaving her behind."

Blaisdel had stayed stubborn but Tom refused to yield, and finally his Annie had ridden in the wagon trailed behind the herd as they made their cautious way north. A couple of Annie's meals, a few days of her quiet presence, and Blaisdel forgot to keep up his complaining. There were other more pressing problems to face.

There were times Tom Whitlow thought he was partnered with a man from the Devil's quarters. Then he would rub the stump of his arm and feel the age in his bones, the sickness in his lungs, and remember what was behind the unholy partnership. Cheap cattle near the Texas border, bunched and starving on poor grass. The appearance of Emmett Blaisdel with a registered brand and less than a hundred head of scrub steers. Blaisdel, looking for an angle, knowing about rich graze far north on a wild New Mexican mesa. Blaisdel, lacking in the ready cash to pick up more head.

So they had pooled together, Tom Whitlow and his nineteen-year-old Thomas Ann and Emmett Blaisdel, a man of questionable ethics but with an energy and drive that old Tom lacked. An unholy pairing, for damn certain. Tom Whitlow had acres of doubts about his partner, and the man's looks did nothing to ease his worry. He had the manners of a tough, rode a powerful blue roan saddled with a Texas rig, stared straight at a man and spat sideways when he was meaning to disagree. Tom Whitlow couldn't right come to what bothered him about the man but he knew it was there, buried deep and waiting.

Emmett Blaisdel was a big six-footer, muscled hard through his chest and arms, with a neck that rolled from his jaw to his breastbone. Straw-blond hair half circled his head; it was rare to see the man without a hat. A bold and clean face with blue eyes and dark brows, wide cheekbones, all diminished by a mouth bowed pretty enough for a woman. It was no wonder Blaisdel affected the fashion of a drooping mustache, but it could not cover the pursing of his red lips.

All in all, Tom Whitlow didn't trust the man. Now, Whitlow knew he himself was nothing special. He could tell a cow's condition from a mile's glance, and a look to the sky gave him tomorrow's weather close enough to live. But he never could put those talents to working for him and his; it was always another man's cows got the benefit, another man's pocket that got the jingle. Which was the cause behind him teaming up with Blaisdel's uncertain temper and tremendous power. It was a late gamble for Thomas Whitlow, and one he took for his Thomas Ann.

No doc needed to tell him; he could feel the rattle in his chest, could taste the copper in his mouth at night, and knew that twenty-some years of riding with an unhealed minié-ball wound had caught up with him. It was now or never for Thomas Ann. Whitlow spat in a cup and didn't check for the rusted stain he knew would be there.

Blaisdel's scheme was simple and clean, touching few lives along the way. The only way Whitlow would deal with the man. Cattle bought cheap, mostly with Whitlow's cash, cattle trailed to a mesa Emmett knew, where the grass was belly-high to a steer's mouth. Grass waiting to fatten up the greedy herd. Then the herd would trail to the nearest railhead, be shipped out, and the profits split even. Blaisdel put up the men and the push, Whitlow put up the cash and his years. It was a one-time deal, a deal for quick money and little risk.

Thomas Ann turned out to be a blessing; she kept the hired cow nurses in line. At least Blaisdel said these men were here to work the stock, but there were faces among them that did not go with riding hot days and cold nights. Whitlow kept these doubts to himself; it wouldn't be long, it would be done in a few more months. Then they would all ride down from the high mesa and be glad to settle and separate.

It was what they were doing to the land that ate into his sleep. The destruction he saw in the overgrazing. He'd owned graze once, for a short while. Acres that yielded tallowed cattle which sold high. He had been careful, for he'd known too many head ruined the land for a long time. It took the fragile grasses of a dry country years to put down roots, take hold, and draw nourishment from the dirt. A greedy steer held too long in one place could tear out and kill acres of the land in a short time.

Which was what Blaisdel was doing with his patterned grazing to this mesa; Blaisdel's quick-moving scheme that put money in their pockets and left behind a mesa ruined for years.

Tom Whitlow watched his child move across the dirt floor, carrying tin plates to a bucket of warmed water. Her face was shiny and high-colored, from her activity and from her anger at the crudeness of Blaisdel's cowhands. Tom shook his head, hating himself more at that moment, knowing all his efforts were contained in this child's sweet smile. And knowing inside him that a wrong such as he was allowing could not truly be justified by a father's concern for a motherless girl child.

There was too much to Tom Whitlow's thinking, and a new edge had been added in the past month. A big laughing man named Teller John, who had come to the high mesa with impressive sheets of printed paper, built himself half a fancy log house, talking all the while of the mansion that would someday replace the crude home. Blaisdel had had words with John, harsh ones that could kill a man. Words meant to back the man down, give them their needed two months. Blaisdel said his piece then rode around the dictates of Teller John, smiling at the man and handling the cattle as if nothing had been said.

Here too, Thomas Ann had become a prize. Tom Whitlow felt the dig of shame in his gut when he tried to avoid knowing the facts. Blaisdel had said the hated words to him two weeks past, and they still bit into Whitlow, still burned his face and soured his belly. The voice grated in his ears as if the words were fresh spoken.

"Whitlow, that-there girl of yours, she comes along right handy now. I seen that Teller John looking at her. Hell, the man's almost old as you but he got him an eye. Fancy dresser and all, guess you might be liking his attention to your Annie. Might get you a rich son-in-law and then you can set back and live your life.

"And for now, old man, her smiling at John keeps the man off our backs. Slows him from doing anything to mess us around."

Then Blaisdel hooked his leg around the horn of his saddle and pulled out a knife, poked at dirt embedded in the base of his thumb. Whitlow wanted to reach up and hit the man, but knew to his deep shame the pride and the strength weren't in him. Blaisdel went on talking as if Whitlow's girl were a prime heifer.

"Yeah, she's a pretty child, your Annie. And she's earning her way right now. Thanks to you, old man, Teller John's off our back."

34

Whitlow had to discard what was left inside him; his pride, his knowing that if he looked to Blaisdel's shaded face he would see what was base and hard in all men. Not enough days had gone by yet that the sore inside him had begun to scab over. Blaisdel's words tore him still, with nothing to ease their sharpness. He could do little more than watch his child, stand between her and the sleep-dulled men who rode in to eat, rode out in a a scattered line. He could protect her only with the money coming to him from the cattle venture. The sleepless nights and the pain in his chest were nothing when he could see the smile on his girl's face, or the light in her when she looked out across ''her'' meadow. From the window her pa had made up special, she could lean on its frame and gaze until her eyes blurred and she had to go back to her chores. For Tom Whitlow those moments were what kept him doggedly moving through the days, kept him quick to answer Blaisdel's questions, quick to offer his own directions for the herd. There would be something left out of this for his Thomas Ann. Something more than a muddied dress and a face worn with years of weathered chores.

He couldn't figure out the sound. A soft, rustling, sweeping noise that came and went with the lurching bed he slept on. It was a puzzle to Blue, one that finally brought him out of the half-dazed sleep. He let his fingers reach over the shallow edge of the wagon, and when they found a fine thinness that ran through his grasp, whispered across his knuckles, he knew what the sound was. Grass, tall thin grass, divided by the wagon's passage and whispering its complaint.

It took some doing, but Blue pulled himself half up in the wagon bed, and the sound of his labors must have reached to the driver, for the team slowed abruptly and the thumping of his backside on hard wood eased up.

''Well, Mitchell. You're awake finally. You've done some sleeping, missed a whole lot of pretty country. My country.''

The driver turned in his seat and looked down at Blue. He had to struggle some to remember the man's name but it

35

came to him, along with a reacquaintance with bruises and tears that came out louder than the man's voice. Blue ignored the face and prodded at himself until his fingers found a surprise that made him gasp. Something passed over the regular features of the driver, and Blue spoke up without much thought.

"Ain't nothing, Mr. John. Finding myself, that's all. And it sure is pretty land. Grass this high, you got a fortune here in cattle feed."

The man winced from the words, but said nothing. Blue took his time to look around. Grass as far as he could see, high-bellied grass come to full ripeness, dried slowly by the high sun. The air held a crisp smell, and there was salt rime whitening the fine black team. No sign of mud to their legs, no wetness at their muzzles. It gave Blue pause. Then he looked over the edge of the wagon, stared carefully at the closeness of the dusty ground.

"Water's scarce up here, ain't it, Mr. John?"

"What makes you say that . . . ?"

"Team's dry. You ain't stopped to water. Grass's too thin. Looks good, but it's too thin. You dry-ranch this land, you take care of it, or it'll die on you. Real quick."

Again that flash of something in the fancy man's eyes. Blue shifted weight on his butt, felt a bruise or two take exception. He was coming up uncomfortable with what was nothing more than a casual conversation.

"Mitchell, for a rider says he's not a rancher, just a drifter, you know a good deal about this land. More than I knew when I came here. And I will admit that surprises me. Pleasantly.

"And Mitchell, my name is Teller John. Not Mr. John."

Blue didn't mind the correction on the name. Fellow had the right to expect his passenger to speak of him any way he chose. But Blue didn't like the approval he heard in the fine voice, or the light in the shiny hazel eyes. As if Blue had passed some kind of a test he didn't know he was taking. Then the conversation on the steps, the words spoken after that ride, came back to him, and he ducked his head, quick to let his understanding show.

"Mr. John, I growed up on ranches, always worked out for my hire. Had to learn something those years. Nothing no self-respecting cowhand don't know, you take the time to ask him."

There was a silence then, as if each man were measuring the other, figuring out the next line of attack and defense. Teller John inhaled a deep breath and let it out, fingered the shiny new reins on the fancy harness. The black team sighed with him, the off gelding stamping a hoof to protest a fly. John let his gaze wander the sight before him: the endless green wave tinted a bitter yellow at the top. There would be three or four more miles of traveling before the destruction became evident, when they crossed the far hill and reached into the more wooded sections of the mesa. It was there Blaisdel and Whitlow had first held the herd. It was there the killing began.

The blue-eyed rider sprawled in the wagon bed saw too much. It had taken Teller John much longer to understand. Of course he had come to the mesa knowing that water was scarce. But he'd had the rights to the spring signed and sealed and recorded in his name at a brick-front courthouse. The spring would feed life to enough ranches, provide for enough families, that there could be a town on the mesa. But the springs would not support the mesa if Emmett Blaisdel had his way.

Teller John almost glanced at the silent man in his wagon; he knew the rider was trying to lean up against the slatted sides, trying to find a spot that didn't hurt. The man looked up quickly, as if to acknowledge what had not been said, then turned those hard-worn eyes away, to look over the end-less green with its brilliant sky that reached way down. The eyes came back once more to rest on John, the long face opening in a brief, almost teasing, grin, and John knew a quick hatred for the man. For his careless knowledge, his ease with the stock, his supreme confidence in what would come to him. Then the surge of feeling passed and John watched the face break into its full grin, the eyes lighten their judging stare. Still Teller flinched when the man spoke, and the team leaned against his hands, shifted in their rattling harness.

"John, now it sure is pretty setting here, watching your world do nothing but shine. But you want to get home, if you got one, before that sun disappears. I'd say you hie up that team, get them moving again.

"Mister, can't you read? It's getting on to dark, and this is purely a lonesome spot to sleep the night.

Rarely did Thomas Ann look out the back window of the crude cabin, to sight on the rutted path that was called a road here on the mesa. It was more usual for her to smile to herself and look out the big window her pa had built for her, to see the life that moved through the gentle meadow sloping down from the cabin's stand of trees.

There were birds she'd never seen before, lots of small ground animals, leaner and quicker than any she'd known. Deer came to the meadow early morning, when they must have known the riders offered no threat. Perhaps they were aware of Thomas Ann's watching, for they would glance over their soft-colored backs to the cabin, nodding as if in general agreement. But they showed no fear, not of Thomas Ann.

She shook her head, and the loose hair that brushed her face was a reminder. No matter what her pa said, there was something wrong in what they were doing here. She had seen the clouds of dust that rose when the cattle were moved. High tan clouds that colored the land. It wasn't for her to worry, so her pa said. It wasn't her place to think on such things. She needed to cook for the riders, and Mr. Blaisdel, and her pa. That was all.

Thomas Ann was a slender girl with a hand-span waist, her soft fullness of figure covered by an aproned calico dress. The loosened wisps of hair were a pleasing auburn, the sunburned and freckled face taken from plainness by wide, slanting, dark brown eyes. She had grown her years to be-

38

come a quiet and thoughtful woman. Dominated by a father turned restless from the loss of his wife and his land, constantly worried about the next day's dinner, the next night's bed, Thomas Ann had left her childhood in the barely remembered greenness of the high Wyoming grasslands and the warmth of her mother's voice, the lost booming of her father's laugh.

Now it was the dulled fear of Emmett Blaisdel, the bitter knowing that her pa was caught in something wrong. The tightness around Pa's mouth, the reluctance of his gaze to meet hers, the vacant stare as he looked at the beauty of the mesa. As if Pa didn't hope for much any more, as if Pa was getting even less than he had expected.

Thomas Ann moved to the low frame that turned out to the corrals. There was dust boiling on the ridge, someone traveling the seldom-used road. She ducked through the door, stepped out onto dried pine needles, and walked to the poled corral. When she leaned on the fence she felt the knobs of rough-cut branches through the worn cloth of her dress. There was someone up on the ridge driving a rig, someone coming past the shabby log hut that was her home.

It would be the man Pa said claimed all of the mesa: Teller John. Thomas Ann had met him several times and thought him handsome and well-mannered. Bowed over her hand, like she'd heard fancy men did back east. His mustache had brushed her skin, tickled her, raised bumps all up and down her arm.

It would be Mr. John; no one else on the mesa would own a rig. She could see the high-stepping team now, the matched sleek black bodies, the new harness gleaming in the streams of late sun. And there was someone with Mr. John.

Pa would be wanting to know if Mr. John was bringing up men to stay with him. Family perhaps, or gunfighters. She'd listened to Mr. Blaisdel talking on what Teller John might do. Pa would want her to watch careful, be able to tell him what she saw.

She took the path to the catch pen, where the riders left night horses. The corner post was loosened. She knew the spotted gelding sometimes rubbed his thin mane on the post: there were black-and-white hairs caught on a rough splinter. She pulled them free, made a loose wispy braid out of their sharp colors. Her fingers were busy with the detailed work.

The close sound of the team lifted her head, as if she hadn't known they were coming along the road, as if she were caught up in her mind with what her fingers were doing. She watched the wagon with unconcealed interest and was neighborly with her shy wave as the team and wagon came closer.

Someone strange rode with Mr. John. Someone Thomas Ann had never seen before. And he didn't look like a friend of Mr. John's. He looked like one of the men who rode for Mr. Blaisdel, one of the silent riders who barely looked at her. She wanted to see this man closer. Thomas Ann stepped toward the road, for it was important for her to see this man. The wagon and team slowed then, as if to accomodate her need.

It was a young face that looked out at her, with heavy blond hair tangled around the bony skull. Bruises stood out on the high forehead, along the narrow jaw. He looked straight at her then, and Thomas Ann could not meet his stare. He was dressed like all the drifters she had ever seen: shirt torn, pants faded to a nothing color. She looked at the dusty ground. What would a man like this be doing with Mr. Teller John? She did not understand.

She would not look at his face again, she would not see those blue shaded eyes. It was the eyes that caught her: they held all the color of the day, the fancy new team, the painted rig, and Mr. John's bright silk. An uneven color, like the color of the shine on the small birds that flew into her private meadow, her quiet world.

Mr. John saluted her then, taking the reins in one hand and bringing the other one up smartly to touch the brim of his hat. The man with him, the man sitting beside Mr. John on the seat of the fancy wagon, that man did nothing more than drop his head quickly, then lift it to stare with those unimaginable eyes. As if he could see into her and know her,

40

feel her trembling. Thomas Ann shivered and rubbed cold hands across her face.

Pa would have to know about this man, Pa would have to hear a description. But Thomas Ann knew there were pieces of the brief meeting she would not tell Pa. They were a woman's business, a woman's feelings that were not part of the feud building on the mesa, not connected to the fancy Sharps and the blunt shotgun she glimpsed resting between the two men as they drove past her.

Thomas Ann watched the bright new wagon move across a high ridge and disappear into a gully. The settling dust blew in swirls and covered her faded dress, coated her hands and sifted into her mouth. She had much to tell her pa, and a half secret of her own to carry with her.

FIVE

BLUE DIDN'T THINK much of the morning's errand. Didn't think much of the horse he forked either. Mr. Teller John had a pretty poor string of ranch horses to his place; then again he didn't have much of a ranch. More of an idea, a big one, full of words that expanded every day. But there were the beginnings of a house, a raw, rough-sided cabin that two surly Mexes worked on each day. They spoke no English, just quick-talked between themselves as if no one else existed.

What they didn't know was that Blue understood most of their rapid-fire words. Understood enough to know they laughed at the man paying their wages, belittled his dream of a ranch stocked with fine cattle, water tanks carefully spread out, good blooded horses grazing in the nonexistent pasture behind the ranch headquarters. Blue could almost agree with their judgments; Teller John was more talk than work.

The bay mare bucked sideways, snorting at a top-heavy yellow flower swayed by a hot wind. Blue slapped the mare's wet neck and cursed her breeding and her sluttish dam. Maybe those two Mex workers weren't off the mark, if this bay mare was any example of Teller John's best-bred horses. There hadn't been much choice in mounts this morning.

It had been a six-year-old bay gelding with a thrown shoe and a suspicious swelling in a tendon, and a tired seal-brown gelding, that put Blue on the flighty bay mare. A high-headed witch with lop ears and a long snake neck, built well through the heart and with good quarters, but a screwy look to her narrow eye.

Blue slapped the mare on the neck again and touched her with a spur. She sidestepped from the pressure, then shook her head and half bucked into Teller John's big gray, stumbled and went to her knees on the rutted center of the road. Good goddamn, but it would be a long day.

Then Teller John started talking, and the day got even longer:

"I realize you haven't signed on to work for me yet. Or that by your own words you are not a gun hand, one of the rough string that hire out their expertise with a pistol. Such as I am certain Emmett Blaisdel and Mr. Whitlow have loaded onto their crew. But, Blue Mitchell, I would like your company today. I have a good deal to show you, and to explain."

The man sure knew how to put more into words than anyone Blue had ever known, and he'd known some windy talkers. The big man didn't know what "straight" meant; he kept trying for his way, offering and circling around the offer and coming back at a new angle. As if Blue were some wild horse to be rattled and penned, distracted until the real reasoning came clear. Blue pushed his hat back on his head, looked up to the incredible clearness of the sky, and then sort of glanced over to Teller John riding beside him. Any direct interest would push the man to talk longer. But the man continued his speech as if Blue had been listening all the time:

". . . so these folks agreed to start a small general store for the few ranchers on the mesa. Bring in the mail when it was convenient, carry some common items on their shelves. Like too many of the settlers up here, they put down roots without clearly exploring the degree of available water. I understand they have been dry for quite some time, and are now hauling in drums of water to take care of their needs. So sad, so little thought . . ."

43

Blue stopped listening again. He was content to ride the mare, find her gait and go with it, watch the richness of the high grass as it gave way to the overcropped stubs. Despite his own reasonings, Blue felt an anger grow wild in him. The mare sidestepped again, from nothing in particular, and her dainty black hooves raised dark puffs of fine dirt as she moved on the short grass of the trail's edge. The anger grew as Blue guided the mare back to the rutted path.

A dark cluster rose in front of them, slightly downhill and nestled at a sloped hill. As they rode closer the outlines of different buildings explained themselves by their shapes, and Blue knew they had come to the ranch that served as the central meeting place for the mesa folk. He set himself deep in the saddle, lifted his shoulders, and loosened his arms. Almost anything could be waiting ahead for him.

He knew full well why John wanted him along; to show off a new man, to exhibit Blue as if he were a prize meant to threaten and bully these folks into taking Teller John more seriously. John was using Blue as if he were too dim to catch the purpose of their ride, of their slow, loping entrance to this dismal collection of slatted buildings and tired horses sleeping in the patched corrals.

Teller John seemed to think his eastern education bought him something no other man had out here; Teller John was wrong. Common sense was born to a man, not educated in him. Blue stiffened in the saddle and the mare jumped again. Blue checked around as they entered the ranch yard, quick to pick up on the number of horses, the number of men.

A hard-driven horse stood loose in a patched harness near a closed wood door. Three horses carrying the same brand were bunched under a broken cedar tree. They weren't mounts belonging to the ranch families; these horses were rigged with saddle scabbards and tied slickers, ropes coiled on the off side. Tough, well-bred horses, meant to give their riders a quick edge.

"We will tie up here, Blue. And I want you to meet William Finch, who homesteaded this place, the first man to come to the mesa. He . . ."

44

Blue wasn't listening. There was a familiar face in the trio of men leaning up to the corral fence. A wide-boned, milk-eyed face that grinned up to him, licked soft lips and spat to the side. There wasn't a name to the face, not one Blue could pull out of his memory, but it was a known face with a back-ground of hard trouble listed to it.

"Teller, you got you some quick talking this time. What the hell you bring us up here for? This is set up for trouble. You fixing to pit me against this Blaisdel's rannies, figuring I can kill off a few for you before I go down? Man, what you got for thinking running around that head of yours?"

Teller John reined in the gray and folded his hands on the silver-capped horn. The ridges of the medallion cut into the softness of his palms and he wiped his hands on each other, as if the motion could remove the sweated dirt grained into the whiteness of his skin.

Damn this man. He was supposed to be nothing more than a drifter, a man who could ride any horse, according to his boast. Which he had made good, and Teller had made a profit. It had seemed easy to use the man's wild streak for his own gain, but this one refused to be set up and used. Teller shook his head, touched his fingers to the pale brim of the fancy hat.

"Blue, I am sorry. I didn't know these men would . . . We can leave now. I can come back later for the mail. It wouldn't be much, there seldom is much for me."

Too late, and too soft. But Blue knew Teller believed what he was saying. As if they could swing the horses around and ride out. It was suddenly past time, and Blue jammed the mare with his right leg, drove her in a half circle that picked up in a short lope, and he almost ran the waiting men down before reining in the mare's eager stride.

The name came to him then, and he used it as a fuel for his anger.

"Buel. Buel Goddard. I know you, mister. Come here looking for a fight, ain't you? Well, this one ain't coming to

45

you free. It's going to be on your own head when you get cut down."

The words were unexpected, and Blue knew enough of the man who used the name Buel Goddard to know that suprises were not his way. Blue had seen the man once before, had watched him carefully set up and take out a boy. A hothead with a big pistol strapped awkwardly to his thin waist. The gun rode high, the boy's hand was wet, and Goddard laughed as he danced the boy with shots spaced at his feet, between his legs, and finally straight to his pounding heart.

That had been some time past, but Blue never forgot.

"Goddard, you can't handle me. Back off your friends. They can't get me this time without taking you along. Think on it, Goddard."

The pistol Blue had drawn from the saddle pocket of the old Mex saddle lay comfortably in his hand, rested across the swell of the rig, pointed right into Goddard's face. Blue watched the white skin turn a fine shade of gray, saw lines strain the wide mouth, sweat cover the heavy brows over the deep-set icy eyes.

A man to Goddard's left raised a hand to his gun belt. Before Blue could speak Goddard shoved the man with his elbow and shook his head, but never let his eyes move from Blue's face. There was hatred in the gaze, caught with a mixture of fear and damaged pride. A look Blue had lived with before; an anger growing fast as the man stared at Blue, memorized the long face, the shining and insolent eyes.

A familiar pattern for Blue: anger tended to turn to Blue's shape and form. It would come back to him one day, when this man thought he could get the advantage. For his anger had gone past the boss's commands to kill or maim Blue, had gone into a revenge for imagined insults, for the bare fact of Blue's face and body.

No matter; for now Goddard was as neutered as a bawling and new-cut steer.

"Mr. Goddard, you pick up your friends and you ride out quiet. This-here's a nice little settlement, and there ain't no

46

place in it for the man you think you are. They don't take to child-killers here.

"You hear me? You ride, now."

Blue let the barrel of the old Navy Colt wander slightly, touching on each of the three men as they untied a horse and swung into the saddle. But he kept the main focus of the pistol on Buel Goddard.

"Ride out. You lost this round, and now I know. And I ain't much on forgettin'. Ride."

Thomas Ann drew back from the rolled-up cloth that served as a curtain on the window and thought hard on what she had witnessed. One of her pa's men had been branded a killer by the odd rider who traveled with Teller John. She had seen the white-faced man ride in earlier with his companions, but they had not come into the small store.

That they had been waiting for the long-haired rider with the strange eyes was plain to her now. That their intentions were dishonorable she would have to accept. What had gone on out in the yard was beyond her experience, but the hatred and the anger was easy for her to read in the four men involved. She knew also that nothing had been solved.

She had told her pa that very night about seeing Mr. John and a strange man riding with him. She talked over the busy heads of the men seated at the table and eating silently, tearing the fresh-baked bread, chewing the sweetened beans and slab steaks. She had told pa all about the strange man, the intensity of his eyes, the quick grin he had given her while Mr. John saluted. She had even described the fancy wagon with its matching team, aware as she did of the distress in her father's face.

Now the thought came to her that was too terrible to accept: that her pa and Mr. Blaisdel wanted the strange man out of the way and had sent these three to take care of the matter. Just as the rider had accused them, just as she feared deep in her mind. She turned away from the window, let the cloth blow over her trailing fingers. She would talk to Libby

47

Finch, she would say bright words to cover the distress she felt.

Then Teller John had come into the small room that served as the mesa's post office. He wanted to ask Mr. Finch about any mail that might have arrived for him. When Mr. John had finished his business, he swept the room with his gaze until he found Thomas Ann, and then he lifted the pale hat from his head and bent from the waist in a deep bow. Libby Finch giggled behind Thomas Ann, and heat flushed Thomas Ann's skin. The voice boomed in the confined room:

"Why good morning, ladies. So nice to have a vision of sweetness and gentle nature in this harsh land of ours. Miss Whitlow, Miss Finch, it is good to see both of you on this fine morning."

She couldn't help stammering, the man was so flowery and almost silly with his own words. But the stuttered sound of her own speaking angered her, and Thomas Ann was curt when she got her voice working.

"Mr. John, what was that about outside? Why were those men here? They didn't come in to the store but waited there by the tree for almost an hour. They were waiting just for you."

Mr. John looked at her strangely, and Thomas Ann was aware that Libby Finch and her father were shocked by her boldness. But she had to know.

"What is his name, that man who came in with you? And where is he now? Who is he?"

When Teller John thought about the events that followed, after all the dust had settled, he shied away from the knowledge that it was that particular moment when he became truly jealous of Blue Mitchell. He had known from the very beginning that the man was a magnet: for trouble, good horses, the confidence of other men, and the shining interest of pretty women.

Becker Sorrell's wife had accepted Teller's casual attentions, yet she had exhibited sympathy and too much curiosity about Blue Mitchell as he sat on her porch steps and bent his head to her ministrations. Teller had not wanted to admit it then, had not wanted to know that a ragged, sun-dried and -bleached rider could hold the women he himself could not.

Here it was again. Thomas Ann Whitlow, who preferred to be called Annie, or Anna when she felt formal, already here she was, taking notice of Blue Mitchell, wondering about him, concerned for his welfare. Teller bared his teeth in a smile and tried to keep his voice even.

"Why Miss Annie, that's a rider named Blue Mitchell. Said he could ride anything, and he proved it about a week past. Surely your pa told you about the drifter who came to Mr. Sorrell's place near Vaughn and rode that wild bronc he calls Thunder. Surely your pa told you.

"And as to your accusations of my complicity in some kind of face-off out there, I have no idea why those men were here or what once went on between them and Mitchell. I was as surprised and as distressed as you seem to be. On the ride home I shall question Mitchell. He is now working for me, to help me establish a good herd of horses and cattle. I wish to bring up the quality of stock here on the mesa. It is my dream, Miss Whitlow. But of course, you are not interested in dreams, only in the hard facts. What I have said is all that I know, Miss. It is to my distress I cannot help you further. I apologize."

Teller hated the sound of his voice, hated the whine hidden between the words, but he knew it didn't matter. Thomas Ann wasn't listening to him at all. She was staring through the grimy window, fascinated by something she could see in the dusty yard.

Blue thought he recognized the girl, thought he'd seen her first at the window when they rode in. He was certain when she came out of the store with another girl, a child really, not much more than fifteen. And there was Teller John walking between them, arms touching the air above their shoulders in the gesture of a favored uncle.

But the look on John's face didn't belong to anyone's uncle. The older girl was sure enough the woman who had waved to them past the rough cabin on the road to the mesa. Blue thought things were complicating up real fine.

Teller John had a rough pull to his mouth, as if something didn't set right. Blue had a feeling all his own; a deep, roiling ache left from confronting the whey-faced Buel Goddard. A high pounding in his throat, a taste of something off in his mouth. But he patted the pistol, returned it to its worn place on the old saddle, and spoke to the mare. He had the horse tied to a tree and he knew he should reload the pistol, loosen the mare's cinch, ease her back. He didn't want to take the chance. He might be having to ride out fast.

There was a lot in this day Blue didn't like, and as he watched Teller John walk toward him with the two girls he had another quick taste of the sourness in his mouth. Then he looked closer at the young women.

The thin girl was a good fifteen; poor color to her skin, hands a roughened red, hair drawn flat to her skull. Blue knew the signs; too little food, poor in quality, too much hard work. He grinned at the child and waited, and sure enough she blushed prettily, gave him a shy smile, and stopped in her tracks.

Then Teller John put a hand to the waist of the other, but he quickly removed it when she turned and stared hard at him. A girl with sense. Blue almost laughed, but swallowed and choked on the impulse.

He liked this girl. Almost a woman, almost her own. Almost pretty, in a different way. He liked the dark eyes, the red-tinted hair, the strength to her face. There was a direct intelligence to her gaze as he stood to her examination. He was used to this behavior, and he knew what would most likely happen.

She blushed, a deep fiery red to match the depth of her hair and bring out her freckles. Blue dropped his eyes from hers, suddenly uncomfortable with what had always been a game to him. For once Teller John's talking was a blessing.

"Blue, I want to you meet these young ladies. This is Miss Whitlow, and Miss Finch. Ladies."

Blue stammered over the expected politeness, words he'd

had little use for in his years. "Miss, I am pleased to make your—pleased to meet you. Both of you."

He would have tried the bow he'd seen Teller John make, but it was an awkward gesture and when he nodded his head and looked straight into Miss Whitlow's eyes he knew he had been smart for once. Something lifted in him then, and he spoke without thinking, full of a pleasant sweetness.

"Miss Whitlow, it surely is a pleasure to meet with you. I remember you, I saw you waiting by that corral fence. Yes ma'am, it is a pleasure. And you too, Miss Finch."

He saw the two young women clearly, and it all came to him then. They were the reasons behind the land, the hard-worked ranchers trying to build what they could. The schemers willing to destroy what would be enough for those less greedy. And Teller John, who fitted nowhere in the puzzle, who planned and laid out ideas and held his money and his education up as a reason to be counted. It was these two young women who counted most.

And then it was back to the dirty and uncomfortable facts of the day. Blue shook his head, angered by the betrayal of his own scattered thoughts.

"Teller, it's time. You got what you come here for, now we best get to riding."

There was more he wanted to say, to Teller John and to the auburn-haired girl with the freckled face and biting eyes. Instead, he tipped his fingers to the brim of his battered hat and swallowed his thoughts, spoke the polite words that were all he could manage. He felt a fool, and knew it showed to the others.

"Miss, uh, Miss Whitlow. And Miss Finch. It surely was a pleasure."

SIX

THE THREE RIDERS moved at a rapid, even pace. Not hurried by success or slowed by defeat. Damn. Emmett Blaisdel knew before the white face of Buel Goddard came close enough to read that they hadn't finished the job. Damn. Three men for one rider. Blessed odds, that should have been enough. Teller John didn't count.

Blaisdel scratched an ear, waved away a lazy circling fly, and tugged at the length of his mustache. He'd hired Goddard to take care of problems like the blue-eyed rider. And the man had failed, first time out. There was no acceptable excuse. Blaisdel waited impatiently as the men rode toward him.

Buel Goddard knew the temper of a boss well, though it was the first time he had worked for this particular man. He rode straight to the rider on the big blue roan and shook his head as he reined in.

"Pulled a gun on me straight out. Never even talked or looked at us but rode up and waved a Colt. Smart son, Mr. Blaisdel. And you're smart wanting him out of action.

"I figure he and that loud-talking Teller John have ridden out to the plains, checking on John's land. Most likely that Mitchell's plumb bored by now, listening to John's fancy words.

"We come back here first to give them time. Too many of the folks at Finch's Corner were watching. Change to fresh

52

horses, then we'll ride out, find those two, and take that long-haired bastard for a pretty ride. Change his mind real fast. That's all I got to say, Mr. Blaisdel.''

If the words weren't an excuse, they did well enough as an explanation. Blaisdel wasn't going to let Goddard off too easy, but he knew he'd chosen well in this man. Nothing much bothered him, nothing rushed his temper or strayed his hand from the given chore. Blaisdel's voice was harsh, his words to the point.

"You know why you was hired, Goddard. Best finish the chore, beat the hell out of that man, and he'll suddenly find a different place to suit his taste. You ride out now, get done. Then we got cattle to move again.''

What he said next was not for hired hands to know, but it was somehow important that Goddard understand. The two men with Goddard, silent through the brief exchange, looked as if they heard nothing.

"Whitlow's caving in, softening to mush. Talks under his breath about this mesa, as if I can't hear. Damned fool. So we got to hurry, we got to make our moves and take all we can. See to it, Goddard. See to it now.''

The morning was slipping from them too fast, and Blue felt a growing restlessness. Even after the words about needing to leave, Teller John had found more reasons to stay around Finch's Corner. Another of the mesa ranchers had come in, a bent and gray-haired man named Fletcher, who barely looked at Blue but got right into arguing with John. Blue gave up waiting and watered both horses, loosened the cinches, and tied them to a tree. He retired himself then, sat on the comfort of layered dry needles under a split pine and dozed. Let Teller John talk and get heated up; Blue could always lean back on the rough trunk of a tree and catch up on some missed sleep.

Light laughter woke him from the timeless dozing. He stayed under the protection of his shapeless hat to watch the two girls walk the small ranch yard. They moved arm in arm, heads bent to each other, giggling and talking. Their gazes swept over to his isolated tree and Blue finally accepted their interest. He stood slowly and the giggling stopped. The two girls were motionless.

It was forward of him to approach them. And equally forward of them to speak with a young man near their age, with no escort of older folk around. It was a breach of unwritten code that left them all uncomfortable. But it settled out between Blue and the auburn-haired young woman, and the presence of the Finch child did little to slow the words passed back and forth. There was a tingling at the back of Blue's neck, a warning of payment to be taken for the pleasure of standing in the sunlit yard and talking of nothing. He would pay; it would be easy, for the girl was special and worth the price.

She loved the land, was delighted by the variety of flowers on the mesa, enchanted by the wild animals that came to her private meadow. Blue listened and nodded his agreement. He watched the dark eyes glow, saw a rich life come to the pale freckled skin, wanted to hold on to the fluttering hands as they tried to encompass a world outside his comprehension. This was new for him, the love in her eyes for something she could never own, never claim as hers, but could love and watch from a distance.

The young woman must have seen something in him, for she asked the right questions, waited quietly for the slow answers, and Blue found himself talking around things he had not known were part of him. The horses he'd ridden, the rough wildstock, the half-broke spoiled broncs, the curious and willing youngsters. They were his life and his love, as untamable and free as the land was for her. The flesh of these endless horses could be used and ridden, groomed and touched, but the spirit in them had no owners and no boundaries.

Time was lost for both of them until Blue felt Teller John's big hand clamp down on his shoulder and he came around in a spin, ready to fight. John stepped back as a knife appeared in Blue's hand. In the moment it took for Blue to know who was facing him he heard the quick intake of breath,

54

the rush of fear from the girls. He let the knife slip back into its sheath, opened both hands to show his intentions, and wanted to apologize to Miss Whitlow, to Teller John, to anyone who would listen. Blue Mitchell knew then he was being pulled by the spoken words into something he did not want, could not handle. He shook his head. It was long past time to ride.

Then Teller John broke the too-bright shining day and left Blue shaking and silent.

"Well, boy, that was quite a demonstration. Now I'm convinced that you're a good companion for me up here. You'll keep me safe from the wild Indians and the rustlers roving this fine land. Nothing can sneak up on you, boy. Nothing.

"Ladies, you will please excuse us? Good day to you both."

They rode out with no more distractions. Teller John led the way at first, in high spirits, letting the big gray gelding run off the morning's idleness. Blue fought the bay mare until she would lope at an easy pace, away from the gray's flank. John finally reined in, looked at Blue, opened his mouth as if to speak. Something of Blue's mind must have showed, for the usually talkative man shut his mouth. They alternated the horses at a trot and a lope for almost an hour, covering the expanse of the mesa at a good pace.

The trip ended in a wide circle ridden across the flattened top of a hill, over land coarsened with stubby juniper and piñon, strewn with heavy rock and broken slabs. As the horses moved through the thick trees, a heavy scent of sweet pine came to the riders. Blue found himself anticipating the smell, welcoming its richness. Then the ground sloped away, tumbled down an incline where a great wave of grass spread itself for miles.

Teller reined in the gray, and Blue let the mare drift to a stop next to the big gelding. Nothing was needed as the two men stared across the wide green basin, but Teller John had gone a long time without the sound of his own voice.

"This is also mine, Blue. All this. I either lease or own

most of what is out there. You can already see that Whitlow and Blaisdel have brought in their scrub cattle. Look at the bare places, the dust. It is criminal.''

The bay mare shifted suddenly against Blue's hand, rubbed her head along the gray's flank. She froze then, tried to whirl around, out from under Blue. He slapped her neck hard and she quieted with a shaking of her head, her ears flat to her neck.

"Teller, you got a claim and a paper for this land, but it don't never belong to you. Use it, graze it, or fence it in. Don't much matter. But it sure is pretty land that you claim a title to. And you're right, you got to take care of the land, build up a good seed herd, and she'll give you back a life-time.''

Blue heard a young woman's words echoed in his; then the bay mare lifted her head and nickered. Blue let his fingers tickle the dent in her neck above the withers and the mare lowered her head and shook her heavy mane.

"You know, Teller, it's going to take a hell of a crew and a good boss to get this land fenced with that infernal barbed wire. Better'n the men you got to your ranch now. And you know, you son of a bitch, that man ain't me.''

They were hard words spoken to a man he'd shared meals with, but Blue was pushed by the ready grin splitting the man's face. As if the harsh sounds were what John had expected. Blue stiffened in the saddle and the bay mare swung her head in tense response.

Teller John let the grin spread across his face. He couldn't much help it; Blue Mitchell was again one step ahead of him, which made him want the man with him even more. He had thought the sight of the wide green basin would be enough temptation, but it seemed to do little more than strengthen him in his refusal. Teller fingered the braided horsehair strings attached to his pale gray hat. Damn.

"John, want you to know, we get back to that ranch of yours, I'm putting the shoe back to the bay and riding out. The brown's had enough rest and the bay's tendon won't bother much with being led. Beholden to you for the hospitality, but it's time I ride on."

Teller hadn't wanted to hear the words, but he'd known they were coming. Known they were inevitable once he sat Blue out here and thought to tie him to the land with its beauty, and the beauty of Thomas Ann Whitlow. He even thought to argue, but a sideways look at the long skull, the flare in the ocean eyes, and he had the good sense to keep his cajoling words to himself.

"Done, Blue Mitchell. It's been a pleasure, though, and for certain you will be missed."

Then Teller stuck out his hand awkwardly across the saddle, and felt the power as Blue surrounded the soft fingers with the length of his own and grinned over the gesture.

"Boys, you hold on to each other right there, real pretty like. Don't move now, or things could get tricky."

Blue felt the shudder run through John at the unexpected sounds, and knew for himself that he was in deep trouble. The voice was Buel Goddard's, and the bay mare swung her haunches, trying to see the horses as they came out of the scattered trees. Her restlessness pulled Teller's gray with her by the strength in Blue's grip.

Then a rope settled over Blue and tightened across his chest, pinning both arms to his sides and freeing Teller from the hand clasp. Blue knew what was coming and slipped his feet free of the old wooden stirrups, not wanting to be caught at the mercy of the mare's increasing worry. When the pull came he shoved himself sideways as much as possible, but the weight of his body and the looseness of his fall spooked the mare and she lashed out at his long frame, catching him on the shoulder and grazing his head with two quick hind feet. He landed hard on his back and slid several feet before the unseen rider at the end of the rope could settle his own horse. The bay mare whickered shrilly in the few seconds of utter silence.

The words went over Blue as he lay sprawled on the ground, dazed by the force of the fall and the touch of the mare's hoof. He could barely understand what was said.

"Mr. Teller John, you hold right still. Don't aim to hurt you this round. But this ranny of yourn, he insulted me this morning, made me look bad front of my men. Got me an obligation to show him his lessons. Set quiet, Mr. John, or you get the same ride."

That would take John out of the picture. Blue suddenly crossed his hand and reached up to finger the slackened rope. One hand slipped under the heavy twist, then the tips of the other hand sought their freedom. The unseen rider yanked back his horse and the rope tightened with Blue's fingers trapped inside. He cursed and tried to roll, but the still unseen rider knew better and kept his horse backing slowly, circling, dragging Blue over the hard ground at a decent walk.

Then there was another moment of relief and Blue tried to free himself, but there were high cries, whoops and yells, someone fired a pistol, the loose rope tightened abruptly, and Blue saw the hard black legs of the bay mare flash by his head. So it began, the nightmare ride across Teller John's claimed graze.

Teller John was making a move to find his pistol when a rope settled over him. The white face of Buel Goddard came up close beside Teller, hands wrapped with coils of the stiff rope. The noose never tightened on Teller but rested hooked on his pistol butt, caught above his elbow on the left side, tugged ever so gently when he thought to move. A reminder that any fool notion of bravery would earn him the same as Blue Mitchell now enjoyed. The fear inside Teller threatened to choke and drown him, and he felt the droplets of cold sweat drip from his face, tunnel down from his armpits along his ribs. He willed the gray gelding to stand still and wanted desperately to close his eyes.

He had to watch; the rider on the rugged sorrel had tied the rope short to the flat horn of Blue's Mex saddle, leaving barely enough room for the mare to run without trampling the tumbling body beside her. Buel Goddard's fine hand was in this, a wicked sense of justice that sickened Teller. The mare ran blind across the high grass, kicking back violently at the inert flesh close to her heels, panicked by the shots and the yells, urged on by a flanking rider when she slowed. Teller prayed that Mitchell had been slammed into unconsciousness.

The end was inevitable in the tree-strewn plain; the mare raced around a wide-based piñon, and Blue's body rolled into the lower branches and was caught, dragging the mare to a stubborn standstill. The flank rider looked up to where Teller sat pinned motionless, and must have seen a signal from Goddard. For he left the steaming mare and the limp body and loped his horse back to the group of expectant men.

A quick flip of a wrist and the rope slipped from Teller's chest. But he wasn't free yet; Goddard swung his horse around, and his words were spoken plain and clear.

"That's a warning, Mr. John. You tell your rider he ain't wanted up here on this mesa. You neither, Mr. John. You leave the herd be. They'll be gone soon enough, and you got acres up here of this grasslands. We all be gone soon enough.

"You understand what I'm speaking to you? Mr. John?"

Then they were gone. Teller bit back a reply, aimed to the dark rump of Goddard's horse, that if they had left him alone, him and Blue Mitchell, Blue would have been gone by tomorrow morning. He had already ridden off the mesa in his mind, it was only the doing that wasn't finished. Teller thought he knew enough of such men that now Blue Mitchell would have to stay. For pride, for revenge, for pay-back.

The rise of emotions in Teller caught him off guard and he almost let a sigh escape. It was to his advantage, the ride just given to Blue Mitchell. But he felt an anger and a deep fear inside him that rolled through, an anger that was tinged only lightly with the pleasure of the thought that Mitchell would have to stay. This was no way to have a man work for you.

Teller jammed spurs to the gray, slid the horse downhill and out to the plain. Goddard and his men were gone. Blue Mitchell still hadn't moved. Teller brought the gray to a stilted walk when he got too close, for the bay mare starting dancing and her lethal hind legs approached Blue's skull.

He led the gray to the mare's head, tied both horses to the

piñon well away from Blue, and cut the taut rope from the mare's saddle as he walked back to the waiting body. He was amazed at himself; he was cold, calm, detached, logical. He knelt and touched the flesh along Blue's jaw. There was a pulse, faint but steady. There was life. Teller looked carefully before touching any other part of the man.

The body was streaked with blood, stripped bare in places from the dragging, pinned with cactus spines, and torn from pointed sticks and hard rock. Teller rolled him gently out from the base of the tired piñon, cut through the yoke of red-soaked hemp, and then did not know what else to do. He stayed near the long form, mesmerized by the slow rise and fall of the exposed chest, awed by the pink-striped flesh showing beneath skin and bone.

Then Mitchell groaned, opened one eye. He tried to sit up, but Teller put a hand gently on the heaving chest and let Blue push against it until his strength gave out and his head lay back on the ground. Teller shrugged out of his embroidered leather vest and wadded it, lifted Blue's head, and made a lumpy pillow for his comfort.

"Godalmighty damn."

The words were spoken in a husky whisper, and Teller didn't know if it was his voice or Blue's. But the eyes opened again and the man looked straight into Teller's face. The leather bastard actually had the beginnings of a grin crossing his darkened face.

"I ain't dead yet. Not yet . . ."

The eyes closed then, the tendons in the neck loosened, and Blue was unconscious. But the few words lit something in Teller John and he finally stood up, caught the gray, and brought the horse to stand near Blue. There was no chance of mounting the man on the bay mare; it would have to be the gray. Teller slid his arms under the limp neck and at the waist. When he rose with the burden he came up fast, thinking to lift a heavy weight and finding almost nothing in his arms. The kid was skin and bone, to be sure. Teller shook his head again and raised the body to lie belly-down on the saddle.

Blue spoke again, and Teller almost dropped him from the fright.

"I ain't goin' nowhere over the back of . . . less I'm dead. Done it once, guess I was dead the.... . . . Teller, you set me up, load me legs-down over the fork. I ain't . . . no horse . . . facedown."

One of those damnable eyes looked straight into Teller's then; the other was sealed shut with swollen flesh. But that one eye had enough in it to silence Teller's protests and draw a strong shame in him. Teller did what he was told and guided the long legs down to the silvered stirrups. He tied the raw hands to the silver horn, bound the shredded boots, even found the man's torn hat and forced it hard on his head for some protection.

He had to look one more time into the bloodied face to see if there was more waiting for him. And as if the wounded man knew what was in Teller's mind, the one eye opened again, the long mouth curved in a devil's grin.

"Teller, I . . . saw. Nothing . . . you . . . could . . . do. . . ."

Then Blue coughed over the effort of the words and tried to spit, but the reddish liquid dribbled from the corners of his mouth and lay on his chin.

"Hell . . . mess. Them sons-a-bitches."

It seemed to Teller that Blue had more to say, but there were no words left. Teller took a careful look at Blue, roped and tied to the gray's saddle, then he looked across Blue to the wide expanse of grass. For the first time there was doubt in him that anything was worth what showed in Blue Mitchell now. The effort of every breath he tried to draw, the ache in every muscle and bone. It was a swell of feeling Teller John had never known before: something close to compassion for another human being.

Then Blue nodded down to Teller, lifted his hands against his bonds as if he wanted to ride on, flailed his legs weakly along the gray's sides. Teller untied the bay mare and climbed aboard, adjusting himself to the unfamiliarity of the old Mex

61

rigging. The gray led quietly beside the mare, as if the gelding knew something about his sloppy passenger.

They completed the wide circle started early in the day, the wide, sightseeing swing around Teller's land. It was almost black when the feeble light of the ranch became visible. Teller guided the mare to the front of the house, slipped from her off side, and cut Blue loose. He held him tenderly across his chest and the man slid free from his bonds.

Teller yelled then, loud enough to bring the sleeping, uncurious men from the crude hut that served as their shelter. The two Mexicans came with them, talking rapidly in their meaningless words. The front door was held open as Teller carried his burden through to what would be a fine living room someday. There was a rope bed in the corner piled with blankets and soft quilts, and there he laid Blue, careful to unfold the long legs and to spread the arms away from the stained shirt.

There was a new vengeance in Teller, a renewed energy, as he cleaned the blood away, wiped the sores, and removed the cactus spines and embedded rock dirt. His hands shook as he worked, and Teller began to doubt his ability to finish the job laid out before him. The man would need more attention that he could give; he stared at his own offending hands, bitter at their cowardice when they were needed. Two of the wounds were great tears that needed stitching. They would have to be tended by someone else. But for now Blue rested quietly, bathed in black salve and wiped clean of scabbing blood.

Teller stopped his work before sunrise and seated himself on the front steps, tasting the cold coffee in his cup. He had a purpose now, and it wasn't until he started on the second cup, this one laced with brandy, that he realized the purpose had little to do with Teller John.

SEVEN

LIBBY FINCH AND her mother asked Thomas Ann to stay with them for a while. All that was necessary was to pass along a message by a rider that she was staying at Finch's Corner. So her pa wouldn't worry. It wasn't often that Thomas Ann had the company of other women, and her pa spoke highly of Mr. and Mrs. Finch.

It was settled; Mr. Finch handed a folded note to one of Fletcher's men, and Mrs. Finch told the girls to run out and play. Libby rolled her eyes and shook her head at her mother's words. As if they were still children, and still played children's games. But it was nice to walk in the sun through the thin grass and bright flowers, to talk with someone close in age. There were some things Thomas Ann did not try to explain to Libby. She was still a child at fifteen, even though she was the oldest of the four Finch girls and carried an adult's load of chores.

There was an older brother, Jacob, who had turned seventeen last week. He drifted in and out of the shabby ranch, always on some mission of unspoken importance. He watched Thomas Ann with his thin blue eyes, followed her at the rare times the mesa had a Saturday barn dance, and his unwanted attentions left Thomas Ann vaguely distressed. But she had asked, and Jakey was out somewhere on the mesa, doing something their pa had asked him to do. Thomas

63

Ann let a small sigh escape her, and planned to enjoy her visit.

Libby had lots of questions about the wild, blue-eyed man who had rode in with Mr. John, who'd rode up to that strange white-faced man Mr. John had brought with him to the mesa. They were questions Thomas Ann herself wanted to ask, but she could not face Libby's curiosity, could not begin to find the answers. So she pretended she was not interested in the girl's relentless chatter about Blue Mitchell, and Libby soon became bored and moved on to other mesa topics.

Thomas Ann walked outside by herself the next morning, delighted to be alone with no chores facing her. A time for her to sit on a warped step and watch the new sun, feel the growing heat, smell the fresh air. Sounds behind her were of the rising Finch family, small familiar sounds of children quarreling, of pans banging on the stove, of gentle touches that began another day.

Then Mr. John rode in on a lathered buckskin horse. Not the usual clean and polite Mr. John, but a whiskered man pale and shaken. His face eased when he saw Thomas Ann, and he guided the tired horse straight toward her. She did not have the time to stand or to greet him properly.

His "good morning" was curt. Then Mr. John explained his hurried errand, his need for her to come with him. It wasn't clear what he was saying, not until he spoke the name Blue Mitchell. Then Thomas Ann stood up and reached her hand to the buckskin's bridle, pulled herself closer to Teller John. She demanded that he repeat his words, and impatience flooded his normally pleasant features. But he did as she asked and she listened this time, heart pounding at the words, head spinning with what must be done.

She did not have to look for Mrs. Finch or ask for her help. The good woman had listened briefly at the open door and was already working through her cupboard, placing in a high worn basket the needed supplies: a needle and strong thread, lye soap, bleached white bandages. Mr. Finch found laudanum in his stores, bought in the spring when Rebecca Finch, the next to youngest, had broken her arm.

64

The sorrel gelding was quickly harnessed and hitched, and Thomas Ann climbed into the seat and spread the reins between her fingers. She looked at Libby and saw the girl's distress, knew that it was the same as she herself felt. The magic name of Blue Mitchell, the ease with which he had scattered Buel Goddard and Blaisdel's men, the gentleness of his bashful words as they stood near the stunted piñon. Thomas Ann forgot her manners and did not say good-bye, or thank you for her stay. But Libby Finch and her mother waved the neighbor girl away, both seeing the strange blue eyes of Mr. John's new man and both holding to a secret sweetness of their own.

The sorrel labored to jerk the wagon into a faster pace. Mr. John was impatient as Thomas Ann struggled with the reluctant horse. She almost told the man to go on ahead, hurry back to his ranch and Mr. Mitchell. But she was too conscious of the impropriety of her telling a grown man what to do. So she tried to hurry the gelding, until Mr. John cracked a leather strap across its broad back and the wagon lurched and bounced on the ruts as the sorrel hurried his step. They kept to a ragged trot for several miles, with Mr. John slapping at the chunky horse. Thomas Ann was relieved to hand the reins to one of Mr. John's men as she climbed down from the creaking wagon in front of the half-built ranch. Her back ached from the trip, her eyes had spots in front of them, the sun burned at her skin.

It was necessary for her to stand quiet, once inside the house. To take a deep breath and let her eyes and mind become accustomed to the dusty shadows, let her heart take in the smell of illness. It was the outline of the body tumbled in colored quilts that steadied her. Thomas Ann told Mr. John to get her a kettle of hot water, a pitcher of cool water, and more rags, lots of them.

She had to distance herself from the long-boned form of the man as she leaned over him to see the damage, as if her hands and her knowledge were not connected to her heart and mind. She peeled back the remnants of the torn shirt, unmoved by the discolored flesh, the stained cloth, the icy dampness of the pale skin. She had seen men mauled before, worse than this one; she had treated cuts and bruises, had even tended one man crushed under a falling horse. And had stayed with him, holding his hand while he died. Injuries such as Blue Mitchell showed her were nothing special to Thomas Ann.

Mr. John had been most accurate in his diagnosis: there were two long gashes that needed stitching. She asked for a bottle of whiskey, and was not amused when Mr. John raised a foolish, knowing eyebrow. She took the bottle abruptly, soaked a rag in it and wiped the needle and the waxed thread through its harsh-spirited wetness. Then she poured more of the liquor on the cut and didn't flinch when the body moaned and stirred, raised a hand to her, cursed softly, and then was still.

The one time her patient almost woke, almost fought her stitching, Thomas Ann lifted the head and let a few more drops of the whiskey run into the mouth. The head swallowed with difficulty, coughed brutally, and a spasm went through the sharp features, twisting the slack mouth. Thomas Ann poured more of the liquor into the mouth, waited a few minutes, and continued her work. The patient gave her no more trouble.

She was startled and lost her concentration when the patient opened one eye, saw her, and smiled. Thomas Ann was not prepared for that smile. She stuttered an order at him to lie back and let her finish. Her heart beat wildly then, her hands trembled, until she touched the whiskeyed needle to the edges of the torn flesh and was able to continue her stitching.

She thanked the Lord above that none of the injuries was serious, at least none of the surface ones. But there could be damage inside, from what Mr. John had told her. It was hard for Thomas Ann not to be angry with Mr. John, hard for her to understand him setting on his fancy horse and watching Blue Mitchell be dragged. She cautioned herself, for she didn't want to speak Blue's name, didn't want to remember his words to her. She wanted to keep him a nameless body on the sweated bed.

But she thought on Mr. John's words, telling her about the white-faced man, the man who held a rope around Mr. John's chest and kept his horse close to Mr. John's gray. It wasn't enough for Thomas Ann. Blue Mitchell would never have allowed Buel Goddard to treat Mr. John so, Blue Mitchell would never have allowed such trouble as Mr. John described.

She pulled herself back to her cleaning, back to the wiping and sewing, and she learned more about the man than she had ever known about another person. Even her pa. This was not the man's first brush with trouble; there was a puckered shiny scar high on his chest, and its mate deep in his back. His hands had the scars of a man who used a rope often, and there were knots and dents on him that came from broken bones repaired beneath the surface flesh.

There was little of the body that Thomas Ann did not touch to bathe, to smooth and check for bruising, to feel for splintered bones. As she tended the man there was an unaccustomed heat in her, and when she looked up once to find Mr. John watching her intently she blushed a crimson red. She became furious when Mr. John had the nerve to laugh at her.

When it was done, she joined Mr. John on the unfinished veranda for a cup of hot coffee and a dried biscuit. She had left Finch's Corner without even the luxury of breakfast.

Mr. John sighed deeply, leaned forward to rest his elbows on his thighs, and stared out past the unfinished corrals to the bright sunlight. Thomas Ann sighed with him, then sipped at the bitter heat and let herself lean back against the rough log column.

"What is your opinion, Miss Whitlow? I am impressed with your skills in there. Do you think there is any serious internal bleeding we cannot see? I worried. . . . What do you think?"

She listed the various sores and black bruises in her mind, felt again the long smooth bone under thin flesh, and shook her head.

67

"I truly don't know, Mr. John. But there was nothing I could feel, nothing beyond those terrible scratches and those two cuts. But they are sealed now, and if they are kept clean . . . I don't know."

She loosened the rein on her feelings, exhausted by the past hours of control.

"He smiled at me, you know. When I poked at him too hard in the—by his ribs, to see if there was anything broken. I saw a doctor do that once and he told me what to look for. The poor man died. . . . He flinched terribly and cried when the doctor touched him there.

"But . . . Mitchell smiled at me, you know. I am not a doctor, Mr. John, and I can only do what little I have learned. He did smile, as if to let me know it was all right. My hurting him so, I mean."

She stopped abruptly, too aware that she was beginning to babble like Libby Finch. Her hands were shaking: the coffee spilled over the lip of the cup and stained the new pine veranda floor. She didn't hear Mr. John get up, nor did she know he stood behind her, bent deeply at the knees, leaning over her shoulder. But she recognized the harsh smell that came from the neck of the brown bottle he held tipped into her cup, and she accepted the gift, understanding the gesture as a common kindness.

It was her first sip of whiskey; she was nineteen years old, and it was her first drink. Papa would say she was on the road to Hell, but Thomas Ann knew some things her Papa did not understand. She let the whiskey's bite soothe her, as it had calmed and nerved Blue for her ministrations. When the cup was empty of the healing potion, she let her head say no to Mr. John's offer of more and was most careful in putting the cup down beside her on the wooden floor. In a few minutes she would ask for the sorrel to be brought around, check one more time on the patient, and then she would go home.

She didn't think of what she'd done as a betrayal. It was nothing more than an act of charity. But her pa refused to see it that way, and Mr. Blaisdel sported a big grin as he

68

stood against the crude cupboard and sipped at his cold coffee.

Thomas Ann watched her papa, suffered with him as he circled in the low-ceilinged room, but she barely listened as he rapidly sputtered the sour words. All about the man who had rode in with Mr. John. The man called Blue Mitchell, who hopefully now lay asleep, and resting in some comfort, after her tries at tending his wounds. As if somehow her going to a ranch and aiding a man sick and torn from a terrible act was only her way of hurting her father. Thomas Ann did not understand; she did not want to understand. But Emmett Blaisdel's cruel grin told her much more than she wanted to know.

She had to turn away from Blaisdel's face and watch her own papa's explosion as his face became a deep and shiny red. She worried about him now, not about his words but about the mounting anger inside him. She would not look again at Mr. Blaisdel, for she understood the peculiar satisfaction in the man's eyes and wished her father could see it and understand its origin.

"Papa, I am sorry if I did something to upset you. But all I did was to help a neighbor, a sick man. Mr. John asked me and I could not refuse him—it would not be Christian. I couldn't leave Mr. Mitchell to suffer alone, Papa. It would not be right."

An act of charity, surely her papa could understand such an act. The fury growing in him was too much for her to accept, and Thomas Ann found herself beginning to become angry.

"Papa, there was nothing wrong in my tending an injured man. You let me take care of poor Charlie Woodson's dying, and I was two years younger then. A child, and yet you left me with his death. Mr. John was with me at the ranch, and his men were there. There was nothing improper in what I did. I have done nothing to be ashamed of. Papa?"

Then the worst came to her, and she spoke out before testing the words in her head. She regretted the impulsive act, but she could not withdraw it.

69

"Pa, maybe you're so angry at me because you know Mr. Mitchell was injured by your partner and that makes you part of the doing. Buel Goddard is Mr. Blaisdel's man, and—"

Thomas Ann flinched and drew back; her father stood before her, white-faced and still, hand raised to strike her in a backhand blow. As if he could hit his own child. Thomas Ann made herself stare at her papa's face, forced herself to keep her eyes still on his. She would not let him frighten her, she would not let him cover her words with such a terrible action.

How could her own papa tell her to let an injured man go untended?

Pa walked past her then, and she heard the gasp as he let out his breath. His back rounded, his shoulders slumped forward, and he stumbled on the bare dirt floor. For a moment Thomas Ann felt a strong pity for the sad old man. He was wrong but he was her father, her only kin in this world. Then he was past her and she began to shake.

A hateful sound followed, and Thomas Ann did not look up, did not acknowledge the noise. It was laughter, cruel, harsh laughter. From Emmett Blaisdel's corner, from the big man who still held a cup of coffee in his hand. Thomas Ann learned the true depth of hatred then and kept her head averted, held her eyes to the stirred dirt floor where her father had paced and yelled at her. She would fill up her head with his remembered words, to hide the terrible sound of Mr. Blaisdel's laughter.

Blue sweated and thrashed the day out and finally woke lucid and clear sometime well after dark. He lay soaked in his own fevered fluids, awake and able to think. The house was silent, with no sign of Teller John or any of his men. Blue felt the wet bedding stick to his skin. He bit hard on his lip when he tried sitting, and lay back to rest a long ten minutes before the next try. He had to relieve himself, and he'd be good goddamned if he'd wet his pants in the stinking bed. Too old for that, too old to be calling out for help.

And too old to lie in the complete darkness and feel tears

soak the gummed corners of his eyes, drench his cheeks, flood his mouth. He sat up this time and swung his legs over the edge of the bed, found the floor a long way down in the dark. Feet wide apart, he stood cautiously, thought for a moment, then made a weaving path to the back of the house, the vague silhouette of the unblocked door frame. He released a stream of urine into the night.

It was a longer journey back to the wet bed, one he'd almost finished when he staggered into a wall and groaned out loud. No one came to his rescue, no one offered a guiding hand to bring him home. He overshot the bed and barely caught its edge with the crease of his butt. It was safety to lie back down on the damp bedding and let his head fall free, his eyes shut again. A long sighing moan accompanied his movements, and the tears came back as soon as his face was nestled in the feathered pillows.

His heart pounded wildly, and he couldn't catch his breath. At the moment of sleep he was brutally assaulted by a new feeling, a consuming and overpowering helplessness. Men rode at him on foamed horses, swung ropes that grabbed him, pulled and skinned him wherever they chose. The ground tore into him, the trees laughed at his passage, the horses nickered and turned away. Forms and figures came at him, passed by him, would not touch him or reach out and help him. It was the force of his own cry that brought him awake.

He chewed the corners of his mouth, raised a hand to feel the lump of flesh that covered his vision, touched his fingers to the hard swelling and let his hand drift down across his chest to the soreness of his ribs. He could feel the prickly sensation of the long cut that sliced across his shoulder, and the three-cornered tear above his elbow. His own flesh, his body, battered and mangled no worse than many another time in his life.

But he didn't choose to close his eyes again, to seek out the relief of exhausted sleep. It wasn't until almost dawn, when there were shafts of gray light to clean out the room of invaders, that Blue could let himself relax enough to let go and sleep.

There was something new in his life, something he did not want. A complete and absolute fear of himself, of his dreaming and his thinking, that kept him rigid and panicked through the long night until false dawn, until he could see well enough to breathe easily. The fear lived hard in him now, deep in his bones, notched in every small cut and sprinkled across the blue-black bruising. He was afraid, and he could do nothing more than turn his head to look through a rough sawed window to the new sun and let the tears drain from him in half-healed paths.

EIGHT

THE NIGHT WAS long for Tom Whitlow. His restless sleep didn't come to him until well past midnight. He lay on the hard-edged cot and felt the core of his hand burning with his near mistake. He could almost feel the softness of his daughter's cheek beneath his hand, and the pain flowed through him. To strike her, to think of beating his beloved child, his Thomas Ann. It kept him awake and tumbling on the bed until he finally bent his knees and left the crowded room, felt his way out of the house and stepped into the magic of Thomas Ann's meadow.

There was no moon, no need for one. Clear air and a full-starred sky were enough light. Tom Whitlow did not look up to the splendor; he moved bent over, cautious of the black-downed pine and scattered rock. He walked slowly until it was smooth grass under his feet, soft and dusted grass that allowed him to sit gratefully on its softness and let his breathing catch up with his age. He had walked a far distance, for he looked back and could not see the small cabin.

Absently he let his fingers touch the broken ground, felt the flow of dirt between his fingers, touched the roughness of the chopped grass stems. Thomas Ann had been right; his child, his daughter of only a few short years, was right in her accounting of his guilt. His rage at her behavior, his untempered anger, had really been aimed at his own lack of judg-

73

ment, not truly at Thomas Ann. It was too easy to strike out at the girl. Much too easy.

He had then let the rage direct itself at a false target, at Emmett Blaisdel and his greed, his smiling savagery in the day's work. But the truth found Tom Whitlow in the brilliant nighttime sky; he could aim the fury at himself and his agreeing blindly to Blaisdel's methods.

Tom Whitlow was not used to thinking inside himself, not gifted with great insight or understanding. He was a cattleman, a hard worker, a paid cow nurse. But he knew his own betrayal this time, he felt the raw deceit in his actions. His one hand went to the aching stump of the loose arm. The gentled tips of the practiced fingers ran light circles on the puckered flesh. He must not forget this, and his body doubled in a tearing cough to send him another reminder.

He owed Thomas Ann's safety and her future to Emmett Blaisdel and his scheme. Blue Mitchell was little more than a corpse now, a beaten enemy to be pitied but not saved. It was Thomas Ann who must dictate his actions; he must not forget her precious face.

The tears came from his heart and bled through shut eyelids. Tom Whitlow bowed his head to hide the shame from no one, and after fifty years of denial gave himself the weak comfort of crying.

Emmett Blaisdel fingered the heavy mustache that covered his mouth. Nothing was working out his way. He slowly unsaddled the blue roan gelding and jerked the headstall free of the big head. The roan snorted and moved away slowly, dried sweat marks bleaching the dark color of his back and sides. Blaisdel hung his gear on a wooden peg and walked slowly to the house, head bent in hard thought.

He didn't consider himself a vicious man, but a practical one. His errand this morning had yielded no results, and now he had to refigure his planning. It had all seemed simple to him, but it hadn't worked out that way yet.

The orders to Buel Goddard had been practical; it was easy to know that as long as the man named Blue Mitchell stayed to the mesa, Teller John would have some backbone to him. Remove Mitchell, and John would again be neutered. But it hadn't worked that way, and now Blaisdel had to find another solution.

He was back from a trip to Finch's Corner, where Mrs. Finch had barely been civil to him when she handed out the mail, and Finch himself turned away from his greeting and took a long time to dig out Blaisdel's order. As if Emmett had done something unforgivable to their nice neat, ordered world. When he looked at it that way, Emmett decided he'd better do some politicking with these folks. They ran the pulse of the mesa, they guided the few ranchers' thoughts.

The whole necessity to be polite, to pick and choose his words, hide his quick feelings, angered Blaisdel more than anything. It came down to the Mitchell rider. Nothing more than a nuisance in the beginning, a grinning and insolent son of a bitch who gave a few folks heart with his easy manner. Now Mitchell was a problem getting out of hand. Blaisdel knew he'd find a different way of dealing with the man. It was a matter of time; he needed only a month longer on the mesa. And a man could completely disappear in that time, not to be found again for years. Buel Goddard would like those orders.

Still, he had tried to be civil about the matter. It was the folks to Finch's Corner who would not let it go. Emmett shook his head at their folly. They had signed Mitchell's death warrant, and the rest was on their heads. He thought of the morning's foolishness and wondered again at the righteousness of some people. Then he settled himself in a crude chair and waited for Buel Goddard to return. The morning replayed itself through his mind.

"Mr. Finch, how do." He'd tipped his hat the way he'd seen that Teller John do, and nodded right politely to Mr. Finch as if the man were important. There had been a flicker of something in Finch's face, but the man's wife showed him only a grim and determined distaste as she listened to him talk. But he'd tried, damn it, he'd tried.

"Too bad what happen between my foreman and that drifter staying to Mr. John's place. Hate to see personal grudges like that spill over on a nice little town like this one. I done spoke to Goddard, he swears it won't happen again. He's real sorry."

The words did little more than tighten the sour look on the old lady's face and deepen the fuss riding her man. Even after Emmett had tried again, looking for better words. Damn, but he hated playing games.

"Don't rightly know what's between them two, but Goddard came back riled 'bout gunplay right here to your store. In front of them children of yours. Said Mitchell rode him down, threatened him bad."

That should have been enough, but the woman glared at him, shook her head wordlessly, and handed him the small packet of mail. It was Finch himself who finally spoke up, as befitting the man of the family. And Emmett hadn't liked the tone of the words. Not at all.

"That white-faced man of yours, he stood here a good hour before Mr. Mitchell and Mr. John rode in. Chased our youngest away, mind you, frightened her to crying. Didn't want no one to talk to him, didn't want nothing to do with us. As if he were too damned—"

The man quit right there, never finished what he was saying, as if it hurt him. But Emmett knew the end of the sentence. Pride it was, pure pride. Something he hadn't thought these hard-lucked ranchers could hold to up here. Goddard had showed his contempt of them, and that damned Mitchell had spoke up real polite. Quick to make friends, simple as that. Buel Goddard had showed his contempt, and Buel Goddard was Emmett Blaisdel's man.

Blaisdel tried again, but he knew there weren't nothing he could do to ease things. Perhaps earlier, if he hadn't sent Mitchell on that ride . . .

"Now, Mr. Finch, you got to understand Buel. He ain't a bad man, just got him a temper and a sense of right and wrong. Buel, he knew that rider from somewheres else. No harm done to the man. I heard he's up and walking, out riding again. See, no harm done.

"Now, even Tom Whitlow, he got feeling bad about the trouble, sent his child over to help. Neighborly of him, that's so."

This was where he really lost Finch. The man drew himself to full height, the thin face rattling in its loose folds and the soft eyes almost getting a light in them.

"Mr. Blaisdel, for one who commands men and cattle, you do not see very clearly. Mr. Whitlow had nothing to do with his daughter's going to the John ranch. She was here, with our Libby, when John came in panicked and looking for help. It was my wife who handed out the medicines and our son who hitched up Miss Whitlow's horse. In fact, I heard that Mr. Whitlow was quite angered that his daughter went on such an errand of mercy."

Damned again. Blaisdel quit at this point. He'd forgotten old Whitlow raving at the girl, yelling and raising his hand to her. Forbidding her to do what she had already done. So Blaisdel paid for his few purchases and left the narrow store, shaking his head at the mix-up of stories left behind him.

So, he'd gone and tried words and explanations and they hadn't worked. Blaisdel never had had much faith in words, but a lot of faith in the hard end of a gun. If Goddard had shot the son of a bitch right off, before the man got known on the mesa, there would have been little fuss. Only the rotted body of a man barely known. Now Mitchell had ridden through the mesa, bought supplies in the store, been shaked and patted and talked to as if he were a favored son.

Blaisdel reached for his vest pocket and found the makings, rolled and lit the cigarette. He let the pleasure build in him, let it wipe out the facts of Blue Mitchell and the dragging for a few minutes. There was a solution to the problem somewhere in his mind.

The deal was turning sour on him, and he couldn't figure it. Whitlow was fussing against him, urging him that the cattle were fattened enough, ready to drive off the mesa now.

Whitlow was a fool. Emmett Blaisdel knew that now. The man had come in with the money and a pretty daughter. They were eating right fine on this venture, but it wasn't enough to smooth out the old man's notions.

There was more: Two of Blaisdel's own men were giving him trouble. Two that had ridden with Goddard over to the wide basin, been part of the dragging. They were worried about that goddamn Mitchell, Blaisdel would bet on it. The rider had an uncanny way of looking at a man, bringing up the anger, or fear, hidden in him. Those two riders were close to fearing, Blaisdel could see that. As if they'd put themselves in Mitchell's place. But it was simple: You rode for a brand, you took the orders. No more, no less.

Then there was Teller John. The fool had started fencing the springs, where before he'd dug out the water, cleared it for everyone's use. Even let Blaisdel's cattle water there with no fuss. Whenever Blaisdel had met the man, before all this misery about Mitchell's wild ride, he'd been polite and friendly, with an obedient set to his manner that suited Blaisdel just fine.

Now the stubborn son had come up to the log cabin and told Blaisdel straight to his face, Whitlow too, with no apologies or sweet talk to the girl, that they were to stay the hell away from his water. Stay off his graze. Get off the mesa. Now.

His words didn't come from Teller John's courage; no sir. They came direct from that blue-eyed son named Blue Mitchell. A man like Teller John never had his own courage. He took it from others.

There were things Blaisdel had to set and think on. So far, no one had come to drive his cattle off. There weren't enough men on the mesa for that. Or guns. And Blaisdel had set Goddard and some others to riding wide circles around the loose cattle—heavily armed circles, with rifles laid over leathered thighs, hands close to loosened pistols. Eyes bright and searching.

No one had challenged them, no one had driven off a single head or faced a man down. Blaisdel knew it was only a matter of time, with time a favor to him; the more he waited and did nothing, the fatter the cattle got. With those odds, he could wait out anything.

Blue wasn't sure what he was doing, but it was working. He kept the mare hard circling to the right. Although she refused, Blue was convinced that she would leave the other horses. Occasionally he could see pieces of Teller John through the dust cloud. He was certain the man was laughing at him, as Blue himself would if he were to stand and watch another man ride a bronc the way he was working this bay mare.

Becker Sorrell's bay gelding still had that suspicious swelling to his off fore when he got ridden hard. Nothing Blue could figure out, no big bow to the tendon but a little heat and puffiness. Time could heal what nothing medicinal could touch, so Blue left the horse alone. Which meant all he had was the seal brown to ride. And Teller John's bay mare. Blue cursed the mare soundly, spitting out the words through dust caught in his teeth. Then he knew he heard Teller John laugh.

Hellfire. All he wanted was to ride to Finch's Corner, see someone he owed a debt, and pay it off. No fuss, no trouble. Blue suddenly stopped the mare's mad spinning, watched her shake her dusty head in confusion as he let her settle. Then he doubled her to the other side, spanked her with the end of the reins until she began her circling. Unwinding her, and him. And it might, by god, work.

Finally he took his chance and straightened out the mare, let her see a clear path away from the corrals and the other horses. She still hesitated, so Blue put the rowels against her sides. She gave a half-hearted rear, then went forward—reluctant, wobbly, but forward.

When horse and rider were out of sight of the ranch, the mare settled into a comfortable lope and traveled as her rider wished. Straight, easy, quiet. There was hope for the crazy bay mare after all.

Thoughts of Finch's Corner returned to him. He wanted to leave a message for Miss Thomas Ann Whitlow—or even better, to find her at the store and talk in person. To thank the young woman for tending to him. More than a week had passed, and he was moving better each day thanks to her careful nursing. Sore, yes, and stiff to one side with all the stitching. And some trouble seeing out of his swollen eye. But his arm and shoulder itched furiously, and Blue knew that for a good healing sign.

He had to thank the girl; there was no more room for excuses. Blue felt a tremor pass through his belly, and yelled into the silence of the new day. The bay mare spooked and broke the flow of her gait, stumbled on the rutted path, and went to her knees. This was something for Blue to ride out, a reason not to continue his thinking.

The mare settled under his hand, and the thoughts came around on their own circle in spite of his protest. Blue was afraid, afraid to ride to the girl's place and give his proper words. Pure afraid he would meet with Buel Goddard again. And back down. The fear was grained in him now, a fear he had never known before. It was slowly destroying him, day and night. Tearing at him, until he could not stand to be in his own company.

The nights were the toughest; sometimes he took his bedroll outside. He'd lie to Teller John, say he wanted the starred sky, the sweet air. Lies, all lies. The stars gave a light, defined the shadows into real shapes. There was no room outside for the men in his imagination to come at him with their ropes and their grinning horses. Their nightly charge was more than Blue could bear.

He rode the mare as she drifted across the land, barely conscious of the distance they had covered. Then the mare whinnied and lifted her head, spun sideways and headed toward a bunch of cattle. Blue slipped partway out of the saddle and caught himself, then hauled on the bridle, but the mare's instincts were stronger than the pain in her mouth.

Before him were three men he didn't know, but three men he recognized. One of them had leaned down from a roaned horse, peered at him as if he were a pinned insect, then frowned and rode away without looking back. Blue remembered that much about the one man. The others had blurred faces and loud voices. He knew them too.

Blue found his hand resting on the pistol shoved in the old holster of the Mex rig. He jerked the hand away as if burned by the touch. Then he steadied the mare, let her keep her line to the three horses. The riders had seen him, had reined their mounts close together and rode with knees touching straight at him. A swelling rose in Blue's throat, a sense of distance separating him from the horse he set. He almost gave in to the need to spin the mare around and run her home. It was only knowing she would not leave without a fight that kept him riding forward.

The three riders stopped; the bay mare slid sideways, reached her head close to a speckled gelding and snuffled a welcome, nipped at the pink muzzle, and then quieted enough to stand still. Blue let the reins hang on her neck and crossed his arms over his chest, as if not bothered at all to be faced with three armed men. Three of the enemy. As if he did not care that their hands were resting on their own weapons, quick to defend themselves against his attack. The sun blazed hot, the air stilled; a horse snorted and blew, another stamped a hoof from a nosy fly. Each man waited, each man was ready.

Bob Walker sat between the two nameless men, conscious of the heated skin of their horses rubbing on his legs, the intimate closeness of each man, what a target they'd make if Mitchell decided to fire. Be real hard to miss two out of three, jammed together like yoked oxen. Sweat beaded and ran down Walker's face and he knew better than to reach up and wipe it away.

Walker was only a few years older than his opponent. He was up from Texas for the length of the drive and bored now with the work, disinterested in the mad fussing and fighting Blaisdel and the man Goddard had brought to them. Walker had come upon the small store in Finch's Corner, had talked easily enough with the storekeeper before all the feuding had started. He enjoyed teasing the oldest girl—Libby, if he re-

81

membered right. Met the son, too, a rough child thin as his papa. Mean, too, from the weasel look to his eyes.

It was a good world up here on the mesa, and Bob Walker didn't take to his part in blowing it wide apart. But he'd given word to Emmett Blaisdel, taken the man's pay, eaten his food. So he would stay. But he would no longer rope and drag a man, to orders. He wouldn't fire on the man setting the restless bay mare in front of him. Not unless the son moved first.

He searched Blue Mitchell's face a long time, using the silence to read for damage. He'd seen the man only once before, that morning in Finch's Corner where Mitchell rode to Buel Goddard and challenged him. Drove Goddard away. Walker had had him a good look at Mitchell then, and liked what he saw.

There was a difference now; Walker couldn't touch on it, but something bothered him about the man. It wasn't the faded yellow bruises, or the stiff way the man rode. It was past the physical badges of the Dutch ride. But it didn't matter. Bob Walker wasn't fighting this man again, not for no one's word. The memory of the man's body on the end of his rope, the picture of that flighty bay mare kicking and running, hauling a wet bundle across the plains, came to him too often, and he didn't like it.

Hell, he hadn't even taken back his rope. Left it wound tight around the man. He'd ridden ten paces from Mitchell, stopped his horse, and saw the man was still breathing, saw the red-stained damage. Hell, he wasn't going to use a rope spotted with another man's blood. Leave it as a wrapping, let Teller John cut it loose.

Bob Walker had hated himself at that moment, and faced the same feelings now.

"You're Blue Mitchell. I got no quarrel with you, no quarrel at all. But you planning to pay me for that ride, for taking the boss's orders, why, I got to fight you. Plain enough."

Walker's red speckled horse shifted weight, pushed away the crowding of the horses. As if the gelding felt something from its rider and responded with nervous anticipation.

"Want you to know, Mitchell, I ain't doing something like that again. To no man. For no pay."

That was as close to an apology as a man could get. Bob Walker shook his head, let his hand ride gingerly on the scarred handle of his pistol. Mitchell sat there on that bay mare and said nothing. Just stared. If Walker remembered rightly, it was the same bay mare hauled the man like a demon around that basin. Man was a fool, riding a flea-brained bronc like that.

The high sun burned into Bob Walker's eyes, and he couldn't see the look to Blue Mitchell's face anymore. He would shade his eyes with his hand, see clearer what was coming to him. But he knew if he moved at all it would become a challenge, and there would be dead men on the mesa. It was in his best interest to sit his speckled red horse and let the sun burn into him, and hope that this Mitchell had more god-given sense than he, Bob Walker, had ever had.

For a moment Walker thought it was all done. A twitch went over the long, yellow-streaked face that Walker knew was his own death. Yet the man didn't move, didn't blink, and the bay mare settled to quiet for a long time. Bob Walker held his breath.

Blue felt the black memory push him, felt the way he'd grown and the life he'd handled come to battle in his gut with a new awareness he'd gotten that one short afternoon.

Then the man on the red horse spoke up and owned his actions on that day. Said real honest he was wrong for the doing, but he weren't going to take punishment for the work. Done to orders, and finished. By god, that was all.

The words eased Blue some. He glanced at the two men who kept their silence, and saw only disgust and anger in their drawn faces. They were the boss's men, they were impatient and ready to fight. Blue choked on what came up from his gut, and would have spat it free but for knowing any move would be read wrong and he would be dying on the ground before the bile in his mouth had soaked itself into the dirt.

Bob Walker cleared his throat; four horses lifted their heads and tightened already tense muscles.

"Mitchell, I say we all ride on. Leave this alone. We're in the same mess; we hired out to some man, got nothing to gain from shooting up each other. You want to fight, I'm ready. But I'd more likely be getting back to Blaisdel's steers before they drift on us too far.

"You understand what I'm saying, Mitchell? You figure it out?"

There wasn't a chance to answer. The bay mare swung quickly, head lifted to stare into the trees. Walker's red whinnied, the rider to his right pulled a pistol and fired in a smooth motion. Fired at nothing. Blue jabbed spurs into the mare, heard her squeal as she jumped almost out from under him. He checked behind him, saw Walker's red horse slam into the third man's mount, heard the sound of another gun fired. The red horse reared back, staggered, and sat down. A crimson stain colored his shoulder. The two unnamed riders circled their companion, the loose pistols slid back into emptied hostlers. The red sat like a dog, bit at the great hole in his body, then sighed deeply and laid over gently, flattened out on the ground, and coughed once. Bob Walker stepped from the dying horse as if out of a stagecoach onto a station-built platform.

Blue straightened the mare, heard his name called, and looked to the sound. It was a slender rider on a chunky sorrel, the rider beating on the sullen horse and getting little more than a clumsy trot in response.

"Blue, are you all right? What happened? That poor horse is dead. Who are these men? What are you doing?"

Thomas Ann Whitlow, riding astride the rough sorrel, red hair loose and flying, eyes wild and frightened. Full of sweet concern. Blue rode to her, caught up the sorrel's bridle, and stopped both horses.

"Miss, it ain't nothing but a scuffle. No one got hurt. It's all a mistake. You don't need worrying about this, Miss Thomas Ann. No one got themselves hurt."

He spoke the words a second time to ease the tightness in

84

himself. And to give the girl time to pull herself together. She patted the sorrel's neck, then tugged at the mare's black mane.

"I don't care about those riders. I know they belong to Mr. Blaisdel, I can see who they are. That's Bob Walker, who's going to live up to his name now. That was one of Mr. Blaisdel's best horses. He'll be mad clear through. And Paco, and I don't know the other man. I don't care about them. They're wrong. Whatever they're doing. I don't care."

Her voice rose; Blue made a hissing sound through his teeth as if to quiet an anxious horse. The girl looked at him strangely, then let her weight fall back into the saddle, closing her mouth on angry words waiting to be spoken. She could see that Blue wasn't looking at her or paying attention to what she would say. Of course, he was watching the other men, especially Bob Walker, who had cut loose the cinch on the dead horse and tugged free the saddle, removed the bridle. The man stood for a moment longer, ignoring the brown-tailed rump swung at him by the man named Paco.

Walker glanced over the swishing tail of the offered ride and seemed to stare for a long time at Blue Mitchell. Thomas Ann looked up then, looked into Blue's pale face and saw its puzzled look. She imagined a challenge sent to him by the man standing awkward on the ground. She imagined a war message passed between the two men. But she was wrong.

There was no end to this. Blue knew it well enough. Blaisdel's men had to fight him; sometime, some place. Not now, not with a woman in their middle. There had to be revenge for that morning's odd humiliation. For a moment, looking into the man's gray eyes, Blue thought perhaps this man was willing to let the incident die its own foolish death. But the other two; they were Blaisdel's men to the finish. They had been the ones to panic and fire; it had been their poor judgment to pull their weapons at nothing, in plain view of Blue and the girl. They would be the ones to expect full payment.

He watched Bob Walker, the man who had dragged and almost killed him. The man who stood exposed and unarmed

85

at his feet. There was no surrender in the man, and no fight either. Only weary resignation. Walker lifted a hand to salute Blue, to wipe at a pesky fly, to scrub dirt and sweat from his face. Blue nodded to Walker, swung the mare, and grabbed the reins of the tired sorrel.

"Ride with me a piece, Miss Thomas Ann. I got some words to speak."

They rode for a long time. The chunky sorrel stepped out in a slow beat and the bay mare was grateful for the company. They rode in silence for almost a half hour, until Thomas Ann found her voice and started asking questions Blue could not answer.

"What was going on there, Mr. Mitchell? I didn't see you with a gun in hand, yet those two men, Paco and the other, they were shooting. At you, I would guess. I'm surprised you didn't shoot back, or that Bob Walker didn't just aim and kill you. He was the one, you know. Papa told me. Walker was the one who roped you and tied you to that mare."

She stopped, as if she had run out of breath and nerve. Blue legged the mare sideways to put distance between himself and the girl. There was nothing he could say to her words. There were no questions clearly asked that he could answer.

"Miss, that was a mistake. Back there. No one meant no harm. Just got a little out of hand.

"And yeah, Bob Walker told me he was the one done the dragging. I knew; I ain't never going to forget that face. But he sure enough didn't want to carry the fight. And me, I don't neither."

Blue looked sideways at Thomas Ann and knew something didn't set right with her. So he nudged the bay mare to a jog and the chunky sorrel was left behind, until the girl slapped the leather ends across the red neck and the little horse made a try at hurrying.

"Wait up, Mr. Mitchell. Blue . . ."

He knew where they were. Recognized the flow and lift of the land. The wide sweep of the curved graze, the tumbled rocks rising to a smoothed, flat point. Blue stopped the mare, and didn't know that Thomas Ann Whitlow had stopped the sorrel beside him.

He was swept up in the memory, and shuddered as if the rope only now settled on his chest, stopped his breathing, bit into his flesh. He could feel the rock-hard land, smell the crushed grass and sage, taste the bitter dirt plowed into his mouth. Time raced through him, and Blue wrapped both hands around the wide core of the flat Mex horn.

Something light touched his arm, and Blue opened his eyes to sweet caressing sounds.

"It's all over, Blue. All done. You told me, Bob Walker said it's done. I heard Pa yelling at Mr. Blaisdel. It won't happen again. Not again, Blue."

She was too innocent to meet a man's passion yet, but born in Thomas Ann was a deep and strong loving, a need to repair things broken. She had seen the signs in Blue before now, the veiled worry, the burned fury. Now the true weight of that day came to her, mirrored in the panic building behind those hard, glowing eyes. She had reached out a small hand to comfort him.

Blue stepped off the bay mare before the girl could touch him again. He tied the mare, loosened the cinch, stared out to the expanse of grass below him before starting to climb the broken rock. He didn't know if the girl would follow, but he had to get at the base of the rock and touch the land, read its evidence.

The trail was easy; torn ground, rolled rock, broken cactus, and trampled seedlings. He found the tree that had stopped him. The rope had burned its mark, sawed deeply into the slender trunk, and the new scar was still a sullen yellow sore. The smell was a balm as Blue knelt and touched his fingers to the wound. The tree had not healed, unlike Blue, whose skin was shiny pink and mottled yellow but sealed over and dried to the sun.

Thomas Ann was there when he stood back up, one hand to her mouth, eyes flared wide open. He thought on the words needed to soothe her, but had no air to speak them. So he

87

stepped closer to the girl, put a hand on each arm, felt the sway of her body between the span of his palms.

But it was she who leaned forward and kissed him, shyly, sweetly, on the bruised flesh of his face. If he had turned slightly she would have touched his mouth. But Blue was motionless, and it was the young woman who had to shift between his hands and bring her mouth to his.

There was no more contact than their lips, but it was the infinite length of a dream that came to an abrupt end when the bay mare whinnied shrilly, and a distant horse answered.

Blue stepped back, let his hands fall, looked to the torn ground at his feet.

"Miss Thomas Ann, you don't . . ."

"Hush, Blue. There's no need . . ."

They spoke at the same time, each hearing the other's words, wishing their own to stop. Then a voice called from the top of the rocks and Blue looked up to see a kid from Finch's Corner waving at them. Finch's son, he thought. Just a kid. The boy's voice was pitched high, harsh and shrill.

"Miss Annie, you all right? Miss Annie, anything I can do? I won't let that man hurt you. . . ."

Thomas Ann waved to the boy, waved with both hands, and yelled something meaningless to him that held her laughter and her pleasure. The boy waved in return, but he did not leave the piled rocks.

The boy was waiting for them when they climbed the rock, seated on a swaybacked paint. His eyes turned wicked when he saw Blue climb out of the scrub first and offer a hand back down to Thomas Ann. It was a familiarity that the boy could not tolerate.

"Here, you. If Miss Annie needs help, I'll be the one to help her. Not you."

The pale eyes were cold, the narrow face pinched and ugly. Blue almost laughed. Jealous, at seventeen. Of a pretty girl his senior and past him in experience. Blue folded his mouth, remembered his own pride back then. But he held to Thomas Ann's hand as she stepped to the highest rock.

Jacob Finch flushed even deeper as he spoke his words,

and hated the smile they put on the rider's face. Miss Annie had no business riding out with this man. A stranger to the mesa, a rough horse-tamer who came up on a brag and had caused fighting and yelling and all kinds of trouble. Jacob wasn't going to let this man take Miss Annie's mind from him. She was his, due him 'cause he was the only male near to her age on the mesa. She was his by right.

That Teller John; he held to take Miss Annie hisself. But no one to the mesa and Finch's Corner thought that was right. Jacob heard them talking, heard their snide comments and rude jokes. Given time, Miss Annie would see the right of Jacob's claim, and she would be his. It was the only way. He would study some on the facts and find a way to deal with this ugly-faced, long-haired, bony-handed rider. There was nothing Jacob couldn't do, if he set his mind.

Jacob allowed the cowboy to mount his silly bay mare and ride back with him and Miss Annie, but he kept the staggering paint between the two horses, slapping and kicking at the poor animal furiously to keep his place. It was a blessing when the rider saluted them at the break to Finch's Corner and allowed as he would head crossways to John's place. Best be getting on back, he said. John might be looking for him. John would have work for him.

But there was no relief when the man rode away, for Miss Annie watched after him too long, kept staring at the settling dust, and would do nothing more than sort of smile at Jacob. She didn't answer his questioning the properness of her riding out with a stranger. He had the good sense not to mention the kiss. He couldn't yet go that far. Miss Annie finally spoke sharply to him, and Jacob knew he had pushed too much.

"For goodness sakes, Jakey, you sound worse than my papa. I am friends with Blue, that's all. You remember, it was me who cleaned and tended him. You helped me get the sorrel ready. You remember that. We're friends, Jakey, that's all."

He wished he could believe her. He hated her words, the pictures they drew for him. He remembered his own shame when he took a fever and his ma cleaned and washed him,

89

tended to him. Her hands on his naked skin, cooling him, soothing him. It was done, and proper, only because he was her son. But Miss Annie were no kin to that man just rode off. Miss Annie had no business tending a man that way.

His thinking spun him in circles; of what he wanted from the girl, of what another man had taken. But he kept his silence and let her ride off to her own trail home, waiting at the crossroads until she was well out of sight and gone. What she had done with the rider was wrong, what she had done today was terrible. Jacob Finch intended to punish her; he intended to tell his pa. And his ma. And anyone else who would listen. Then it would be her own pa, yelling at her, and they would chase Blue Mitchell off the mesa.

And when Jacob offered to forgive Miss Annie's sin and take her to his wife, everyone would see the rightness of it, especially Miss Annie. So Jacob let the paint slow to a walk, and let his mind wander through the future only he could imagine.

NINE

IT WAS ALL too much for him. Thinking addled his mind, put circles in what he knew for facts. But this damned mesa; it gave itself to thinking, caught up a man in its problems, pulled him across its beauty with the wide green grass and deep clear sky.

It wasn't Blue's nature to set hard at a problem, work on thoughts that wouldn't hold still to be rode. He could read some, and figure simple numbers. There was even a book wrapped in oilcloth in his saddlebags, dog-eared and worn, and learned by constant reading. But he'd do most anything before thinking too hard on a thought.

Which was what had got him up on the mesa; first by his bragging he could ride any damn horse, then by having to prove on his words. That got him partway up the slow climb to the mesa, all the way north and west from Vaughn. Then he stepped in it by taking up Teller John's offer of a ride in the fancy courting buggy, a ride not knowing where they was headed, and not caring much.

All that brought him to now; riding across the mesa, seeing by the damaged ground where Blaisdel and the cattle had been stepping on the world. Dust scurried around the mare's anxious feet and mounds of half-dried manure cluttered the ruined grass. Blue held the mare to a walk, conscious of too much mixing inside him.

He'd left the girl, Miss Thomas Ann, at the short road to

Finch's Corner, with that whey-faced kid. The boy had a wild-haired look to him, but Miss Thomas Ann smiled at Blue's worry and let him know she was safe to ride in with the kid. He would do for her protection now; Blue could ride back to Teller John's ranch.

It was a good ten minutes of riding and thinking before Blue caught on to the time. It was late afternoon; shafts of sunlight mixed in the low scrub piñon, long shadows spooked the bay mare into stepping high over black air. They had ridden a piece today, he and Miss Thomas Ann. Far from the short moment when he'd faced Bob Walker and the two nameless men. Blue shied from the clouded memory; the bay mare stepped sideways. Riding with Miss Thomas Ann, time had been nothing at all. Blue shook his head, felt the slap of long hair on the side of his face.

She was a special one, Miss Thomas Ann Whitlow. She had seen into him, had taken the fear and brought it back to him in a sweetened kiss. She was pure special.

Too special for him, and too good for that snot-nosed kid riding along with her now. The picture of the boy's sly face was strong enough that Blue hauled in the mare, spun her back toward Finch's Corner for a few strides. Then sense cut through the immediate rage and he was able to settle the mare, step down from her, and go through the laborious process of rolling and shaping a smoke. It wasn't until he'd taken the first drag that he knew he didn't want the taste in his mouth. He ground the stained paper under his heel.

Blue remounted the mare, guided her back toward John's ranch. A hard lump rode in his belly, and he tried spitting it clear of his throat. He was knotted and bound with all the thinking. Piles of words he did not understand. Doing was his nature, not pounding over loose-ended thoughts and possibilities. It was Teller John's ruined graze that was the problem now, not the lump in Blue's throat, or the sweet breath and clear smile of Miss Thomas Ann.

The mare stumbled, went to her knees, and Blue rammed his chest on the flat Mex horn. The mare came up under him, snorted loud, and swung in a restless circle. Blue opened his eyes and looked around him. Pitch-black nighttime, pure darkness. Hell, he'd been riding blind and didn't know it.

He gave it up then, got down and stripped the mare, hobbled her and offered a cupped handful of water from the canteen. She slobbered and licked his fingers, then caught flesh and bit him properly. He cuffed her head and she laid it gently on his shoulder, then rubbed vigorously, almost knocking him down, until Blue hit her again on the neck. The mare went to busily grazing at the sparse grass, oblivious to the rider and the cold night air.

Blue chawed at jerky strips and sipped at the stale water, then leaned his head against a wind-smoothed stump and found himself back at serious thinking. It came easier to catch on Teller John's problem than to look at the darkness facing him, the fear climbing into his unopened heart. He grabbed at the thinking on another man's problem as a relief from his own new one. It took him most of the night to find something. He was tired and hungry come morning, but he had the tail of an idea. As far as he could see, the solution was pure simple. Something to do, something that would bring the action Blue craved. Something that would shift his thinking from his own loss and the face of Thomas Ann Whitlow. His own survival would follow.

Blue grinned as he unfolded his legs, then grimaced at their cold stiffness. His ribs ached again, an echo of the old bruising. He felt the pull of his mouth when he stood, an awkward shape in the early false dawn. The bay mare lifted her head from a late night's dozing and spooked at Blue's approach. He bridled her quickly, loosened the hobbles, and walked her to his gear. Hot coffee, a biscuit or two, and maybe some of the eggs Teller John had coming from hens he kept to his ranch. Then talk, and finally some action.

He grinned again as he mounted the mare, laughed at her cold-backed bucking, and finally let her run in the new sunlight back to John's ranch, back to the beginning of different days.

* * *

The traitorous thought came to Teller John at a weak moment, and he stopped in the middle of the unfinished house. Then he walked on through the half-framed doorway to stand on the wide-planked veranda.

It wouldn't take much to move him out of here; pile up the few belongings in the fancy wagon, harness the high-stepping black team, and go. It would be a shame, for the land was perfect, beautiful, more than enough to fill a man's lifetime of dreams.

He reached one of the rough chairs and sat, let his hands rest comfortably on his knees, while he stared out across what could be the ranch yard. Teller was conscious of having sat in almost the same spot a week ago, when he had shared the early morning and the veranda with a tired Miss Annie. Daughter of his enemy, savior of his hired man. The faces confused him, kept him seated and bewildered.

It was all right, fine, nothing much. He was used to quitting. Running on to somewhere else. He'd done it all his life. But it was different this time, as if the long-haired, wild-eyed rider had been given to him as a second chance. Teller snorted at the convoluted process in his brain; he'd started out to use Blue Mitchell, to squeeze the man's insolent vitality and take it for his own. Then the core of the vitality had disappeared, Teller had been left with nothing. Now he worried about being fair to the ragged drifter.

It had been easy to see the difference in the man after the dragging, the look in his shocking blue eyes, the silence in the long hands. Mitchell shied away from exposed contact with people now; the fine eyes had a rapid blinking, the hands a vague shaking. The dragging had taken something from Blue Mitchell, something Teller John had come to count on.

Teller sighed deeply, wished he had the energy needed to get up and find the almost empty bottle of brandy back inside the house. He looked around, morosely hoping to find awake before his time one of the men he'd hired to work, one of those unremarkable men whose faces were still a blur to him. There was no one in sight. The orders this morning had been to leave off working on the spring, drop the barbed wire in coils near the fence posts, and get to working with the Mexes on the ranch buildings. Teller wanted something to sell, if it came to that point. Neither of the two cowhands had complained about working with Mexes—a bad sign, a sure sign of their intent to do as little as possible with those orders. Teller should fire them. Yeah, fire them. Sometime today. Sometime.

There was no noise in the air, no hammers, no saws tearing wood, no muffled cursing in English or in that rapid, undecipherable Spanish. They'd all disappeared. He was alone. And Teller didn't like being alone.

If he thought much more, he would begin to worry. Mitchell hadn't come in last night. Rode off early morning on that dumb bay mare after stirring up enough dust in the yard to choke anyone setting on the steps, saying he had some things to do. The man rode out with no further explanation. And he hadn't come back.

It was Mitchell's absence that had Teller John setting on his new steps, thinking on giving up. Thinking on how easy it would be to ride out in the packed wagon tomorrow, to travel on toward any place he chose, with no thought for what he left behind. Or who.

It wasn't that he was afraid of Emmett Blaisdel and his men, it wasn't that he could still taste the snug rope drawn over his chest, the pull that had kept him motionless as that bay mare took Mitchell on a ride across the plains. But land and cattle, they weren't worth a man's life. That's what Teller John told himself; nothing was worth a man's losing his life.

What he wouldn't say to himself was closer to the truth: It was his life he was thinking about, not Blue Mitchell's, nor those of the nameless men working for him. His own life; it came down to that basic fact, and Teller John was afraid.

He looked up at the sounds, surprised by their intrusion. A horseman coming across the yard, a bay mare stirring up a cloud of thin dust. It was Mitchell, of course, and there was something different to him, something around his eyes as he hauled in the sidestepping mare and shook his head free of his hat, wiped his forehead with the faded sleeve of his shirt.

"Morning, boss. You got any coffee? Biscuit or two'd set real fine."

Son of a bitch.

Teller made up a fresh pot of coffee as Blue helped himself to the crude kitchen workings and fried up a pan of eggs, heated two stone-hard biscuits. It was almost an hour before the two men got back to sitting on the veranda steps, tin cups in hand, coffee pot resting between them. The bottle of brandy had been found and killed a willing death. It was time for the talking.

"Well, Mr. John, I got me some words to spin out. You got time to listen?"

It was as easy as that. Teller John forgot his plans to quit the mesa, stopped worrying about Emmett Blaisdel and Tom Whitlow. Even was able to ignore the odd remaining doubts on what he'd seen in Blue Mitchell's face the past mornings. It wasn't there now, and Teller wasn't going to push his luck. He sat and listened, that was enough.

"You know, it come to me so simple, I got plumb ashamed having to spend the whole night thinking on it. But, I ain't noted . . ."

Mitchell took another deep breath, sipped at the hot coffee. John was fascinated.

"Your trouble is Emmett Blaisdel, and old Whitlow, and their damned eating cattle. They is tearing up the ground here. Ground you got a rightful claim to, best I understand."

Teller nodded, irritated by the man's slow-started reasoning.

"Raid the herd, scatter the cattle. Drive off the horses. Come in and raise hell with the critters and be gone before they can figure it out. Like I said, real simple."

It was too simple not to have some effect on Blaisdel and Whitlow and their scheme. Run weight off the steers, get the riders spending all their time chasing cattle, roping up loose

96

broncs. Keep them off balance, and Blaisdel would finally throw up his hands and quit the mesa in disgust. So simple.

Teller looked sideways at the long-boned rider sitting near him, sharing the rough boards of the veranda steps. The loose frame was relaxed, the hands stilled around the cold tin cup. There was an ease in the man, a flash of high humor in the odd eyes.

Teller made a big show of thinking on the idea; he rolled his eyes and wiped his hands together in dry relief.

"I don't know, Blue. What you're suggesting is against the law. And I am not one who goes much against the law. Do you *think* . . . ?"

That was the word that got it all going; a brightness flared in the blue eyes and Teller knew he had found the mark. He dug in his point.

"Blue, do you really *think* . . . ?"

A progression of thoughts raced across Mitchell's face—anger, suspicion and doubt—then a blaze of laughter flashed across the other's face. Blue Mitchell appreciated a good joke, even if it was on him.

Thomas Ann had gotten home at dark that day. Her pa had nothing to say but his face was grim and tired, as if he had been hard-pressed. When she took the sorrel to the corral Bob Walker was there, scraping dirt and blood from his gear with a long knife. He was pleasant to Thomas Ann, offering to unsaddle the gelding and see to his night feed. There was nothing said about the incident earlier in the day, and Thomas Ann was relieved. Perhaps Walker had enough strength to keep the other men quiet, perhaps the horse's death would fade quickly.

There was no sign of Mr. Blaisdel or his other men in the cabin, but Thomas Ann knew they would come in hungry and tired. Wanting their supper, half of them readying to saddle up and ride for the next watch on the cattle. She hated Mr. Blaisdel, hated what he was doing to her pa.

The explosion of feeling inside her was a surprise. Thomas Ann stopped in her kitchen chores, breath taken by the strength of her rage. Blaisdel's greed left no one untouched on the mesa. Her fingers found a rotted spot on the potato she held, and she threw it hard against the wall. Then she went to her knees to pick up the splintered pieces, shocked by the violence of her act.

It wasn't until the following morning that her father knew what had happened, that word came to the meadow of her actions the day before. She had to listen to the mesa's version of the events, spoken from the bitter mind of her father. That she had interfered with men's business, that she had brazenly pushed herself between Blaisdel's men and the rider who challenged them. It was Thomas Ann who was responsible for the horse's death, as if she had actually pulled the trigger.

But the worst of the spreading tale was her behavior after the incident. That she had been seen riding with the man, Blue Mitchell. That they had walked their horses close together for a long time, had stopped, and she had put her hand on the man's arm. Shamelessly, wantonly. It had been Thomas Ann who had kissed the man, offered herself up to his evil caresses.

Thomas Ann made herself stand in front of her father and accept his tirade, but she barely listened after the first accusing words. A core of despair held her; it had not occurred to her father that someone had spied on his child, that someone had followed her while remaining hidden. That she had done nothing more than ride with a man, and kiss him. As her father had once done with his wife while they were courting.

Thomas Ann looked at the steaming red face of her father, saw the mouth open and shut around the condemnations, but she stopped hearing the sounds of her misdeeds. He went on and on, and she didn't listen.

"Have you anything to say, girl?"

"Yes, Papa. May I get back to supper now? The men will be in soon to eat. It is almost dark."

She turned away, icy-calm and collected, already back to preparing the meal. She would not let her father's words wound her; she would not let him see the hurt.

Tom Whitlow saw the rigid back, the head held erect and

slightly tilted. He would have cried for what he knew then was lost. So much like her mother, so much strength and goodness. Tom Whitlow understood then; he had given up his claim to Thomas Ann and her affection. Her love. He had doubted his own flesh and blood, taken another man's word above that of his daughter.

Tom Whitlow felt the loss keenly. He could see the broad face and big frame of Emmett Blaisdel, and he felt the bite of hatred. The man was destroying more than Teller John's precious grass. The man was drawing lines between father and child, and he, Tom Whitlow, was the worst offender. He, Tom Whitlow, had allowed the man to lead him easily.

The taste of his own betrayal soured the old man's belly as he took the slow steps across the rough dirt floor to the crude doorway. He had been here before, late at night and repentant, but he had not learned his lesson. The knowing now weighed on him deeply, and Tom Whitlow went out to the cold darkness to chew and swallow his own frail pride.

TEN

He roped the seal brown out of the corral, and told Teller John to pick a dark-coated horse, not the big fancy gray, whose color could be seen far across the plains. What they were doing wasn't legal, and Blue felt the knot in his belly turn and roll, the knot that couldn't be laid to supper's gassy beans.

Unusually quiet, Teller heard him out, and caught up a dark buckskin. His belly fluttered in anticipation. He'd easily gone around the law over the past years, but always with words, intentions, small actions. Not like this, not actually holding a rope in his hand and choosing a mount that would not be seen in the nighttime. Teller shied away from thinking on the actual doings of this night and worked on saddling the buckskin in the pitch black.

It was simple, it had to be simple. He would put his trust in Blue Mitchell, let the man lead him with his planning. Much easier this time to follow than to make a decision. Teller reached under the buckskin for the off cinch too fast, and the nervous horse spooked, kicked out. Teller stepped back, stumbled as a shod hoof scraped his wrist. He slapped the buckskin, cursed it and himself, then steadied the horse and leaned into the warm hide as he reset his gear.

Mitchell had insisted: no fancy rig tonight, no bright reflecting silver or rattling bit chains. A good plain rig with a dulled bit, a bridle tied up with rawhide strings. Nothing that would pick up light or make noise. Teller had snorted at the instructions, then thought on the knowledge and how Blue had come by it, and thought again on his trust in Blue. It was as if the rider read his thoughts, for the long face opened then in a grinning smile, and the odd eyes flashed a deep blue.

"Teller, what I says to you is pure and simple common sense. I ain't no robber or thief, no rustler for the hell of it. But I know what can be seen at night, almost got myself killed once 'cause I didn't think on it.

"You listen, Teller. What we're doing ain't pure thievery but practical survival. It's your land. There ain't no law up here. Blaisdel's herd is ruining you. The man won't listen to your reasons, and neither will—"

He'd almost spoken the name, almost put the sound in his mouth and shoved it out. But somehow he couldn't list Thomas Ann's pa in the cursing he and Teller got a hold of. It would be like cursing the girl herself to speak so of her pa, and Blue found it rough still to think on her connected to the cold-blooded Blaisdel. As if there had to be a reason, an almighty strong and good reason for a man with a child like Thomas Ann to be working into almost full-time thieving. For that was what the cattle were doing, stealing grass, and the future, from Teller John and the other ragged ranchers on the mesa.

Blue kept his mouth silent around the Whitlow name, and looked away from John's face, as if the man saw his omission and would think less on Blue for his protecting the girl. Blue scowled at the brown's thick mane; too much thinking, too much worrying over things that floated in the air and had no body, no skin, no feel and touch to them.

It was a relief to be saddling up to ride. There was no room in Blue for vague thoughts. Action rode the night, and Blue welcomed its anticipation, let its tension run to the ends of his fingers and lift the brown's head in nervous response. Blue looked over the old Mex hull and watched Teller fumble with the cinch, knowing the same tension was in the boss man.

It was time. He mounted the restless brown and waited for Teller. The big man let his horse drift up to stand beside the brown, and for a moment there was nothing in the night but the animals' breathing and the sweet fresh wind, the cool bite of the black air.

Blue loosened and checked a pistol in the saddle's holster. Teller half freed his rifle under his leg, slammed it back tight into the scabbard.

"Hope we don't need any of this hardware, Teller. But we got to protect ourselves if something comes at us. That's all—nothing we aim to hit unless it comes right to us yelling and firing to kill. You understanding what I say?"

Teller nodded, then realized that by listening to the order and accepting it he had given away any claim to being boss of the ranch land, the high mesa, tonight's raiding. Given away the title and the responsibility to a long-legged, loose-minded bronc fanner with no past and no immediate future. Teller sighed; there was an enormous relief in him, as if he had passed on a major burden.

Suddenly Blue reined his gelding in a quick spin and headed out of the yard; the dark buckskin leaped sideways and followed. Teller gathered his reins and set himself, wanted to scratch at the flat place between his shoulders he could never reach, and instead tugged his hat down real tight. It could be a wild night's ride.

There was no set plan to the night, only an idea that followed both men as they rode from the silent ranch. The darkness had settled out to a comfortable warm gray, and it was possible now to make out the shapes of the scrub piñon and the high corral fence. The brown horse snorted with each dainty step, gathered himself under his rider's weight and was ready for any move, any command. The buckskin pinned his ears and flashed his tail, half bucked, and pulled for more rein. It wasn't much past ten o'clock when Blue let the horses step out into a long trot.

They traveled in silence for a half hour; the horses moved easily on the bunched grass, and Blue let his mind float in the dark. There was no destination yet, only yesterday's knowing of where the herd was and the instinct to find them.

Blaisdel seemed to be ranging the cattle in a wide circle, holding them in each place until the ground was bare. His circle had as its center the mud-brown springs that Teller John's bit of paper said were his.

Small signs told Blue they were headed right: fresh-torn branches on the piñon, dark droppings, the smell of dust heavy in his nose. He aimed the horses northwest, remembering a small basin rich in sweet grass. A perfect place for the night's adventure; a place ringed with piñon, threaded with juniper and struggling bent cactus. A place that would fit his plan.

It wasn't much of a plan. Ride in, tie up the horses, strap a thong around their muzzles to keep them quiet. Creep from tree to tree like Indians, get close enough, pinpoint all the riders. Then sound like a deviled banshee and scatter cattle and men all over the mesa. Blue even added a bit that pleased him: If they could, they'd mount and join in the chase, ride with Blaisdel's men and keep the cattle scattered.

It was a real loose plan, but it was something. Blue dropped his hand abruptly; Teller John pulled up his horse, let it drift in beside the brown.

"Hear that? Cattle, whole goddamn herd, not too far ahead. You must live all right, Mr. Teller John, for we've found the steers real quick."

Blue slid from the saddle and disappeared, and Teller spooked, felt cold panic hold him. But then the man appeared at the head of the buckskin, taking the bit in both hands, looking up at Teller. Now more accustomed to the starlight, Teller could almost see Blue, the hard whiteness of the crazy eyes that shined fanatically in the soft gray light.

"Get down, Teller. We walk from here."

Teller dismounted and dropped the reins, couldn't find their ends, fumbled at the horse's bit until the gelding threw back his head and shied, and the reins slapped Teller on the face. He grabbed at them, patted the wet neck, tied the horse to a tough young piñon. He let Blue work the rawhide around the muzzle, below the bit; he let Blue tie the leather tight enough that the horse would be discouraged from a friendly nicker. Teller didn't want to ask where Blue had picked up that particular skill. "Just common sense," the man would say.

A hand touched him on the shoulder and Teller jumped. He could see the tall shape now drifting through the thicket of trees, and Teller knew to follow. He stumbled often, grabbed a tree, and cursed when his knuckles were skinned on rough bark. Moving in the dark, twisting through the stands of piñon and juniper, was hard and unexpected work. He had to keep his head down to watch the footing, he had to look up and sight on Blue's dimmed shape, he had to avoid the branches and spines waiting to stick him while he looked somewhere else.

The muscles in Teller John's leg began to twitch and rebel, the backs of his thighs ached, his feet turned and rubbed in the high-heeled boots, and he began to curse the night and everything around him—including Blue and his ill-defined plan.

When they stopped at last Teller could hear the sounds of the cattle; the soft lowing, loud calls, bodies brushing and rubbing into each other. He stood for a moment, flooded with relief. Whatever they were to do, it would be now, right ahead of them, only feet away. He wanted to cough and spit, to clear his throat, but the soft night air would carry the sound and betray them. Teller choked on the bile flooding his mouth.

Then a hand pushed him on the shoulder, sending him partway around and to the right. Teller looked back, saw Blue's long body fold down in absurd proportions until the man almost disappeared. Teller hunched over then, feeling the strain in his knees, the shaking deep in his belly. He dropped his head, forced himself through the piñon. Slowed, stopped, waited.

No signal was needed, no prompting moved him forward. A coyote called, too close to Teller for it to be real. The sound raised the hairs on his neck, even though he knew it had to be Blue Mitchell. The single note of the false singer was joined by other real ones until there was a loud and eerie chorus behind the one man's voice.

The cattle sounds stilled, and Teller heard a man curse, another man join the first. A steer bawled loud enough that Teller knew he would be trampled in the next minute. The coyotes quieted. The riders, known by their length on horse-back, the Texas crease to their hats, rode past the tree where Teller hid. It was quiet, almost peaceful.

Then the hell broke loose, the hell created by the one-man band. The coyotes sang in pairs and triplets, a nervous steer had a fire-hot branch spanked across its tender nose. The fire sputtered and went out, the steer lifted its head and shuffled from the painful branding.

Teller could smell the steer's nearness, could hear the nervous bowels pour out on the ground. He found courage, and spanked the steer with a knobbed branch. The steer bellowed at the insult and lumbered into a run, eager to retreat from the haunted place.

Teller saw a second burning knob land in the bunched steers. He waved a broken tree limb and swiped two steers across the rump. The coyotes howled and the herd took off. Teller laughed with excitement, knowing no one could hear him above the crazed noise. The herd bunched and split, steers angled off and leaped the broken cactus, slammed into knotted juniper. They bawled in their terror and burst through the waving, yelling cowboys to find their freedom across the wide grass plains. Teller howled with them in pure pleasure.

A hand touched him then, and he jumped ten feet, spun around, and saw the white teeth and bright eyes of Blue Mitchell. He let the laughter grow inside him then, and held out his hand in congratulations.

"Move it, Teller. Quick, get to your horse and ride."

Teller was lost, caught in the sameness of the piñon scrub. He spun and turned, only to almost run back into the spilling herd. He moved directly away from them, as much from blind panic as good sense, and ran into the deep-branched trees, head low, back bent, arms in front of him to save his face.

He heard the horse before he saw him; heard the violent

snort, half strangled by the rawhide cord; saw the dark-tailed rump turned toward him. He had time to step sideways before the buckskin kicked out at the enemy. Teller reached the horse's head, slipped off the rawhide, and untied the reins with sweat-greased hands. He caught the horn as the horse circled and broke into a run, swung himself into the saddle, and leaned over the buckskin's neck, urging the horse to go full out.

Blue was ahead of him, standing high in the stirrups, heading his brown into the scattering steers. Teller saw the man pull out one of those old pistols from the saddle holster, and let his own hand find a weapon. He fired over a small bunch headed by a rider and was delighted by the splintered flight of the steers. He heard Blue's old Navy Colt fire once, then Teller fired again, losing three head for a hard-pressed cowboy almost directly ahead of him.

The man turned and looked back, and Teller thought he could see the white face, feel the man's anger, as the cattle split past the racing horse and were gone. He yanked his buckskin across the herd, splitting a large bunch of almost twenty head. The firing of his pistol doubled their speed, and Teller laughed.

A large bug went by his ear, too close, leaving a stinging touch on him. There was a loud explosion, and the buckskin leaped. Teller grabbed for the horn, knowing as the horse tried to put his head down and pitch that someone was shooting at him.

He hauled on the reins, dragged the horse's head up, and spurred the horse breaking to the right, running from the herd into the dark, into a safety hidden somewhere. The horse lowered down and put everything into running, with Teller perched over his neck, lashing the wet barrel with finely woven reins.

Horse and rider flew into a wide, treeless depression where the buckskin reached for longer strides. It came to Teller that there was no sound following him, so he yanked on the buckskin's mouth, trying to slow the racing horse. The gelding did not respond but put his heart into running from the terrible noises still too close behind him. Teller pulled on the bit until he thought the horse would surely fall, but the buckskin kept running.

Then there was a shape beside him, a dark shadow that matched the buckskin's strides, with a rider crouched in the saddle, eyes white and wild, long hair whipped into a straight line from the tied-down hat. The brown bumped into the buckskin at the shoulder and knocked the racing horse out of balance, slowing the long running gallop. The brown bumped again and again, until the buckskin was traveling in the right direction and Teller could feel a response at the end of the reins.

He almost fell from the horse then, when the shadow spoke to him and the words echoed in his ringing mind.

"Pull up when you can. We got to walk these broncs in cool and dry. Can't leave no sign. They got to be dry, we got to curry them before we get our morning coffee. Don't want any of your hands to think these two been out doing something they ain't supposed to. You know, Teller, them men of yours, they ain't to be trusted none. They'd as soon sell you to Blaisdel as drink your whiskey."

Two miles from the ranch, by Teller's cautious guess, Blue reined the brown gelding to a walk, and the buckskin was willing to follow. The tired horses walked side by side, reins slack, heads low. The riders whispered automatically, as if someone could see and hear them. The words were more than a satisfaction to Teller John.

"Them steers is scattered from here to yesterday, Teller. And we got ourselves free anyway. We go again tonight, 'cause they won't be figuring on us coming so soon. We got to stay up today, work outside, let those gents you call hands see us working. You got another dark horse you can use tonight? That buckskin won't go again, neither will the brown."

The man was talking as if everything the night before had been a success and tonight would be an easy repeat. Goddamn him, goddamn his insolent assumptions. Teller almost opened his mouth to speak, then let his fingers touch the burning on his ear. He found blood.

107

"They shot me, Blue. Shot at me and got me, by god. Nicked my ear. That's too close. Yessir."

Blue ignored the implication that Teller had had enough. Teller hated the man at that moment.

"Yeah, ride again tonight. A few coyotes talking and them steers will remember, run like crazy. It's started now and we can't quit. Not if you want anything left of your basin after Blaisdel and his men pull out."

The two horses quickened their walk and Teller could see the humped shapes of the ranch buildings, the high walled line of the corrals. He felt his ear again, finding that the blood had quickly dried and left only a small scab as witness. He looked again at Mitchell, saw the excitement contained in the odd face and body, and knew a flare of pleasure in his own soul. A high, as if he'd been drinking fine whiskey and kissing sweet ladies all night. Only better somehow, more addicting.

"I think I understand, Blue. We'll go out again tonight. But no more having folks shooting at me. I'll bring a gun, but I sure as hell won't use it unless I must."

The day stretched out long and hot, and Blue's eyes grated under dry lids. He scrubbed at his face, spat through parched lips. The night had been long, and he wanted to sleep. But they would have visitors sometime today, and he had to be working when they rode in the yard. It didn't matter that Teller was in the house, stretched out like a swamp rat on his bed. Teller John was the boss, he could do what he pleased. And sleeping through part of the day was Teller John's habit.

Blue spent time with Becker Sorrell's dark bay. He saddled and rode the gelding around the corral, worked him some off a long rope, watched the chancy leg with a practiced eye. The horse moved straight and even; Blue was pleased. Then he caught the bay mare, roped her close to the raw snubbing post, and sacked her lightly with a loose blanket. He laughed at the bewildered look to her eyes, the loose flopping ears, as she humped and banged around. As if she'd never been worked before, never seen a man or the striped woven blanket, smelling of her own salted sweat.

Simple tasks needed doing; tasks that took only part of Blue's attention. When he put the mare away he was satisfied that she stood almost asleep when he waved the blanket across her face, slapped it high between her hind legs, tucked it neatly under her tail. The witch stood still, one hind hoof cocked, one eye disinterestedly watching his actions. Maybe something would come of the day's work.

He caught up the bay gelding again, wanting to recheck the tendon. He was kneeling at the horse's front end, hands gripped on the leg, when he felt a shift in the bay's muscles and guessed they finally had their visitors.

Blue stood up slowly, leaned his arms on the solid back and watched the riders whirl into the yard, come to a halt, bunch up, and then walk their blowing horses to where Blue stood. He had a pistol tucked in the waist of his jeans and it poked into his sore ribs, gathered sweat and dust along its barrel. But when he saw the faces of the men riding at him he was glad for its presence.

It was the white-faced man who spoke first, old Buel Goddard himself, even though Mr. Blaisdel was at the head of the tight group.

Buel Goddard wasted no time on politeness;

"You sky-eyed, crazy son of a bitch. What makes you think we'd let you get away with anything so goddamn crude as running our cattle last night? Takes a crazy man to think up a scheme like this one, and you are the son to do it. Mitchell, step away from that horse. I want me a clear shot."

The threat was almost as if Goddard had learned from meeting Blue at Finch's Corner, almost as if he judged to ride his man hard and push the issue to a fight. Blue drew in a deep breath, let his fingers touch the heated metal of the pistol against his belly. He'd known they would come storming in; he hadn't guessed that Blaisdel would turn Goddard loose.

Fear bit deep, awakened by the challenge. Blue let the breath go from him, took another, raised his arms and folded them on the bay's wide back, rested his chin on the cross of his bony wrists.

"Goddard, you got a wild hair up you, sure enough. But you got to give a reason when you threaten to kill a man. This ain't your place, you remember that? It belongs to some nice respectable folk who would have questions for your boss there, he lets you slip the leash too far. Think on it, Buel. You want to give up a meal ticket easy as this, and your own life, for the satisfaction of gunning down an unarmed man?"

Pure bluff, pure gamble that none of the riders could see enough of Blue to know if he carried a pistol. A bluff that drew sweat across Blue's forehead, sweat that trickled down the side of his face and itched in the blond stubble of his day-old beard. Blue doubled his fist, looked to the blanched face of Emmett Blaisdel, and forced a smile to his face, put a fire in his eyes. Knowing all the time the trouble those eyes had gotten him into before this. He grinned until his jaws ached then winked at the man, taking a rare pleasure from the fury reddening Blaisdel's jowls.

"You got something to say, Mr. Boss Man? You and your men, you may run your own army but you still got to live with the ranchers up here. You ready to have them come together, maybe call in a law after you?

"You think on it, Mr. Blaisdel, sir. No one's told me yet what I done to bring down Goddard this time. Other than riding stock for Mr. John and visiting his neighbors, I ain't done much yet to anger a man. You want to tell me what's going on?"

He maybe rubbed the words in a bit strong, for now Blaisdel's hand wandered close to a carved, pearl-inlaid pistol, but Blue kept the wide and innocent grin to his face, tilted his head as if asking the question again in silence, and waited an extra beat of time in complete silence.

The click of a hammer being drawn brought all heads around in unison. It was the unmistakable figure of Teller John, legs spread, hatless, outlined by the raw lumber of the veranda. The man held a fine rifle in his hands, and the weapon rolled up and took aim at Blaisdel's chest. The riders stayed motionless and Blue stepped away from the bay gelding, drawing the pistol from his pants and holding it loose in his fist, barrel pointed down. His eyes were on Buel Goddard, and the man knew it without taking his own eyes from Teller John's threat. The loud voice was unmistakable in the deadly quiet.

"You got a problem with Mitchell, or any of my men, you come to me, Blaisdel. Now, what's got you sweated up on a beautiful day like this one?"

Blue let a sigh escape him; Teller John was playing the role perfectly. There was no sign of sleep in his face, nor any other indication of the night's activity. The small nick on his ear had dried clean; there was no trembling of bad conscience in the hands that cradled the rifle. The man would do this right.

Blaisdel spit his words.

"Our cattle got run off last night. Some son of a bitch thought he was playing coyote and run off the herd. Them steers went a good five miles 'fore we stopped them."

The man swiveled in the saddle and stared directly at Blue, noting the pistol hanging from his hand and remembering Blue saying he was unarmed.

"You ain't got the truth in you, Mitchell. You run off them cattle, god curse your hide. You got to pay."

"Mr. Blaisdel, I been here all night. Got to sleep, got up and worked. Mr. John, he can vouch for me. Been working the stock, just like I get paid to. Nothing much I can say, but you're wrong about me."

Between the shine in the green-blue eyes and the easy weight of the fine rifle from the veranda, Emmett Blaisdell knew he had nothing this time. He made the motions of checking on the horses in the corral; several of them bore saddle marks, with the bay mare covered in fresh-salted rime. The gelding Mitchell hid behind had marks on him, as did a brown and a big dark buckskin. Any number of horses showed the signs of a good day's work. Or a night's hard ride.

Blaisdel cursed. There was nothing he could get hold of

111

and shake. And it wouldn't do to kill Mitchell outright, not in front of Teller John and the two sullen ranch hands, the silent Mexes. Too much slaughter even for his hard-skinned men.

"Mitchell, you had you a warning. You ride cross me again, you're dead. I don't care about anything but you staying to hell out of my business. You hear me, boy?"

Blaisdel saw the grin widen on the long face, saw the pistol being shoved back carelessly in the jeans' waist. He had to admire the man's sureness, the man's guts. Just as he had to kill him. Then the son reached up and tugged at his blond hair, and the grin widened more as he nodded over to Buel Goddard. Blaisdel wasn't certain Goddard could hold his temper, and he stiffened for the trouble sure to come. Teller John must have seen the same thing, for the rifle barrel shifted and lined itself on Goddard's shirt front, right on the center button between the loose black vest.

"Don't. Don't. It's certain who dies this time, Goddard."

A small shock settled in Blaisdel. It had been Mitchell to speak the words. As if he cared about the living and dying of an enemy. Goddard eased his weight back in the saddle and Blaisdel felt an ache in his jaw, tasted the bite of blood where he had chewed his own flesh.

Damn. He'd been right in the beginning. The smiling, insolent son of a blond rider was trouble for him. Hard trouble still undone. Right now was not the time to finish this. He cocked his head to Teller John, lifted an open-fingered hand, and waved a wide circle to his men.

"I'll give you my own warning, John. Anyone chases cattle again, there'll be dead men on the mesa. You hear me, you listen good."

"And I'll give it back to you, Blaisdel. What happens to your cattle is of no concern to me. But I will not let you threaten any man who works for me on a whim of yours. You got troubles with coyotes, you put out more guards. Or get them damned cattle off the mesa.

"I don't care, but you will not threaten my men. You hear that, and you believe it."

112

The riders were gone, the dust almost settled from their passage. Blue still held to the bay gelding, leaned on the solid back. Teller John remained on the veranda, alone, the rifle cradled across his chest. Blue could see sparks of light on the high polished barrel as Teller's chest went up and down rapidly.

The man was catching his breath, like Blue was trying to do. Easing back into the day, testing that both of them were alive. Blue broke into the heavy silence by leading the bay to the corral and turning him loose. He took a long time hanging up the halter and the coarse lead rope, made extra certain the big gate was latched and secure. He wanted his breathing steady and even before he faced Teller John.

The man was still there at the top of the rough steps, but he had finally, carefully, rested the rifle against a pillar. He was rubbing a hand up and down each arm, as if the rifle had strained his muscles. John looked out at Blue then past him, staring to the brilliant blue of the sky. He opened his mouth as if to speak.

Blue got there first, guessing he didn't want to hear what Teller John would say.

"Hell of a bluff. You got them. Those sons are still shaking their heads, trying to figure out what went wrong."

John's mouth shut with a click and Blue took the steps in two jumps to stand beside the man. He could smell the acrid stink and knew he gave off the same rank sweat.

"We ride again tonight, Teller. You be sure you pick out a different horse, anything but that gray. Us coyotes will ride again in full voice."

Blue knew that if he thought too much about it he would never head out to the corral after dark. But if he pushed Teller into going he'd have to ride along. It was all more than Blue wanted to have circling in his mind. He shut down his thinking and almost rested a hand on Teller John's shoulder.

ELEVEN

THEY RODE LATER the next night; Blue on the bay mare, Teller on a rugged gelding. The large, restless herd was easy to find; Blue hunkered on the ground, lifted back his head, and howled to the dark moon he couldn't see. The coyotes had a good thing in their nightly song. It gave lift to the spirit to sing to the sky. Blue let his hat fall, closed his eyes, and howled again. Even Teller John got into the act this time and began his own tentative song. But he stayed glued to his horse, a light maned sorrel, and suddenly found himself forking a wild bronc when the gelding tried to run from the unseen coyote's voice. Blue would have laughed, but he was having his own hard time catching the stirrup on the bay's rig.

It took only the first rising howl for Blaisdel's men to gather in their horses, pull out pistols, and rein around to hunt the duo. They didn't fire blindly, for they knew the cattle would run from any noise. But the cattle were primed, and they ran. One man pursued the dying calls of the human dogs, and Blue and Teller led him straight across the mesa top, tangled him in dark piñon-and-rock-covered ground, and finally watched the man circle back on himself, curse, and give up his chase in disgust.

They agreed that it had been a good raid. But they both knew such pleasure wouldn't come easily again. At sunrise in the morning they sat and rested on the veranda step, sipped at bitter coffee, and waited for the rest to happen. The high of the night's ride had worn off, and Blue felt the effects of another night without sleep. He yawned and stretched, heard knots crack in his bones, and knew he wanted nothing more than to find a shady tree, roll out a blanket, and sleep until tomorrow came.

"Teller, we got to do it different tonight. Them boys won't let us near the herd again. By now they got them steers caught up and Blaisdel's on fire, he's so damned angry. But he won't ride in here again, not in broad daylight."

He fingered the frayed denim stretched over his knee, pulled at a white fringe circling a new hole. A few more weeks working for this man, he'd be riding plumb naked. Blue coughed, wiped his fingers across his eyes. A shudder ran through him, and he clenched and unclenched his fists.

"He can't take his men away from them critters tonight. Every mother's son will be out there riding. Blaisdel himself, and maybe even old man Whitlow. We won't be welcome out on the plains again."

Blue's voice faded. Teller shifted weight on the tenderness of his buttocks. This night-riding was getting to him, soring him in places only his mother knew existed. He glanced over at Blue, wondering what the man was working up to in his mind. A highly convoluted mind, capable of outrageous thought.

Teller was surprised; despite the residue of yesterday's standoff—the acrid taste in his mouth, the twisting in his gut—he had so far enjoyed their outings, liked the flirting with danger. Once he got over the scare of having an unknown son of a buck fire at him, actually take a chunk out of his bodily person, he'd found the nighttime raiding a secret pleasure.

"What say we ride over to Whitlow's cabin tonight, pay them a neighborly visit. Show them we ain't meaning no real trouble, show them we just got ourselves a real worry about the land."

Teller's head came up, the words rang in his disbelieving

115

mind. Blue continued talking as if they were musing over the weather's vagaries.

"They got themselves a good herd of horses penned in them corrals. And I'm thinking, tonight, them horses will be by their lonesome. No men to the cabins, sleeping out their night."

There was a long silent pause, while Blue thought back over his words and Teller John knew a moment of complete madness. Mitchell was insane to think of riding into Blaisdel's encampment and raiding his stock. To consider such an idea. It could wipe out a man's sanity, if he were to dwell on it long enough.

Both men looked at each other, saw the mirrored grin, raised their tin cups in silent salute to the coming night's new adventure.

She had never seen one man so angry. Furious. Thomas Ann thought that Mr. Baisdel would burst and die right here in front of her, standing in the low door frame where he had gone to listen to the speed of a rider outside.

Even his back showed the anger, and when he turned from the door and walked into the hot kitchen Thomas Ann kept away from him, frightened by what was in his face.

He shoved a battered cup at her and she poured the coffee, was relieved to have to turn away and put the pot down on the stove. Her pa came in the small door beside her, stopped when he saw Emmett Blaisdel's fury. The two men each stared at Thomas Ann, as if she were somehow to blame for whatever terrible thing had happened. Then they went back through the low doorway, out to the busy corrals. No one had spoken a word.

She could guess; it would be the rider, Blue Mitchell. And Mr. John. It could be nothing else, and Thomas Ann was suddenly very frightened. Only Blue could have done something hard enough to provoke the anger in Mr. Blaisdel and her pa. Her hands shook, her eyes watered, and she bit her mouth to keep the lips from trembling, the tears from falling.

It was in her now. She liked Blue Mitchell. She liked everything about him, everything that bothered other people. She thought she could see more in him than the others did. Thought she could feel and touch the hidden gentleness that was reserved for horses and other wild things. The orneriness that was tamed by the fear in a trapped horse, the sudden break in temper that was softened by the touch of a new-born foal.

She knew all this about Blue Mitchell by instinct, having known nothing more than the sweet touch of his hands on her shoulder, the smell of his warm breath across her cheek, the shudder of his rigid body when she'd kissed him.

Alone in the kitchen, in the silent cabin, standing still in the heated room, Thomas Ann blushed. A rush to her head, a lightness numbing her heart. And the blossoming fear in her, that grew to overwhelm her. They were going after Blue Mitchell tonight.

Then pa came back inside and shook his head when she tried to ask her questions.

"Girl, hush. You don't want to be knowing anything. You get up supper, make us a pot of coffee. Boil it hot and thick. Going to be a long night."

Then, as if her pa knew even those few words said too much, he put a finger to his lips and shook his head at her again, made a hissing sound she remembered from her childhood when she got all excited and pa tried to calm her down.

"Thomas Ann, you hurry now."

They had ridden out well after dark. All of them. Not even Pa stayed behind to protect her. She was alone in the heavy log hut. There were chores for her, mending piled in a corner of her small room, bread to be kneaded, the dirt floor to be swept clean again. Endless chores.

Thomas Ann poured herself a cup of the thick coffee the cowboys preferred and pushed back the canvas cloth that served as a door at the front of the cabin. She sat down on the rotted sill, held the warm cup between her hands, and stared at the land spread out before her. A quiet, still, dark night, with the stars almost in reach. She leaned her head

117

against the grainy wood of the framed door and let her eyes follow the heaven's light.

Blue wished again he'd left Teller John at the ranch. The man was an awkward thief, a clumsy raider. Blue had meant for them to go quietly once they'd tied up the two horses, to move carefully across the years of dropped cones and broken limbs, to walk silently over the slab shale and loosened rock. Blue heard the cursing behind him, the crunch of stumbling feet, and did his own cursing under his breath.

It was a guess Miss Thomas Ann would be in the cabin, and he didn't want to involve her in the raid. It was a matter of reaching the corral fence, finding the slip gate that would be near to the house, and slowly, quietly, sliding the poles to expose the opening. He would wait then, hope a curious horse would snuffle at the sudden freedom and step through the gate, draw others with it.

Horses were strange beasts; he might have to go to the other side of the pen, slap a few dusty rumps, to get the herd moving before they found their escape. Then he would re-stack the poles, leaving the top bars down as if carelessness had loosened the gate, not Blue Mitchell's hands.

It wasn't much, but turning horses loose didn't take thinking, only stealth and surprise. However, if Teller John kept up his stumbling and muttering, both the horses and the lady to the house would know of their intent.

He wondered about the girl, what she thought of the past days' madness. Wondered if her pa talked to her at all. If she ever thought of him at night, when the air was soft and fresh, the day's sounds muted and at peace. Blue shook his head, knowing he was gone past anything possible. He was a drifter, a horse-breaker, a rough string doctor good for only a few more years. He had no life for a girl the quality of Thomas Ann.

He stopped, and was almost prepared for Teller John bumping into him. He caught the man's arm, clamped his fingers hard around the muscles, and felt Teller stifle the cry in his mouth. Blue whispered the words, hoped the man

118

could hear and understand. He sometimes doubted Teller's good sense.

"Keep the corral between us and the house. No good the girl sees anything she has to give to Blaisdel. Quiet . . . Watch for the gate poles."

Something must have gotten through to Teller, for the man's footsteps now had little sound to them. Blue let his fingers tell him where the gate was, running them along the midline pole. It took him longer than he expected to find the gate, and he had to wait then for Teller John to come up beside him, move away from the hand signals to the other end of the poles' ten-foot spread.

The poles slid out easily, made no scraping noise as they came out of the doubled posts. Blue couldn't see Teller; he lifted the first pole and forced it down, waiting for John to bring his end, hoping the man knew not to drop the pole. The four rails that followed were laid in a small pile on the ground.

A snuffling noise startled Blue. He held his breath, listened, saw the shape of a curious horse stick a nose past where the gate had been. He stayed rigid, hopeful, while the horse stepped closer to the dark escape. A shape moved in the shadows, an arm lifted to wipe something from a blurred face. Blue cursed and the cautious horse took one step back, stopped, and stretched its nose to the invisible, enticing line.

Then the horse made its decision, walked confidently through the open gate, hesitated, kicked backwards, and loped into the dark. It was less than a minute before the other horses followed. Blue grabbed for the corral fence, pressed himself into the ridge of poles, coughed in the dust stirred by the excited herd. Dark shapes, splashes of white, a brightly colored paint, a blanketed Appaloosa, a light-tailed sorrel, a bald-faced mare, two grays in tandem.

The horse herd was gone; Blue coughed again, spat his throat clear, and motioned for Teller to follow him. The flash of light that was his answer dropped Blue to his knees. Another shot blasted the night. Blue saw a glow at the cabin, heard a voice calling in the night.

Thomas Ann. He answered her, called her to stay inside, away from the fire. Another bullet whined over him, closer this time, close enough to burn fire across his shoulder. Blue ducked lower, stuck his fingers to the burn, felt the course of blood overrun his hand, soak into his shirt, thread down the coldness of his chest.

He lifted the damaged arm and felt no tearing, hauled at his own pistol stuck in his waistband. A shot rang close to him; Teller John returning the seeking fire. A flare of light and sound came from distant juniper. Teller John must have seen the flash for he aimed straight to its center, and Blue heard the strangled sound of a man wounded deep. Blue froze, cocked his head as if to hear the sound better. There was nothing more; no high keening sound, no flashes of gunpowdered light. Only a liquid moan, a faint rattle, from the dark stand of juniper and piñon.

The thin sound shoved Blue out of his crouch. Experience told him to watch out, to circle the trees, be ready for a trap. But then the moan died slowly, and Blue could not wait. He ran crouched low, conscious of a shadow on his left moving slowly, another shadow that swept past him and hurried into the damning trees.

He knelt to the wounded man, touched the shoulder of the shape beside him and knew it was Thomas Ann. There was the crack of a breaking branch and a tall form stood behind him. Teller John. Blue heard the catch and release of a pistol, the deep sigh as Thomas Ann held out a candle and Blue put a match to it. In tight silence they examined what lay spread out in front of them.

One of Blaisdel's men, left behind for the bare chance of such a raid. A familiar face, planed and angled by the flickering light, darkened by the red hole high in his chest. Blood pumped quickly from its core, and Blue put a hand over the ugly wound and pressed until he groaned with his own answering pain. Thomas Ann looked at him then and the pain was worse.

"It's you. I knew, I guessed. . . . Look what you've done."

As if they'd shot first, as if they weren't only fighting back against Blaisdel's greed. They hadn't opened fire, they had returned the shots in self-defense. Teller had fired the true shot; Blue had done little more than free his pistol and hold it cocked and ready in his hand.

Nothing could be said. Words meant nothing, but the life of the man sprawled out before them had a remaining strength and purpose. Thomas Ann lowered the candle close to the slack face, and Blue didn't know if the sound he heard came from her or from his own shocked mind.

The man shot and downed was Bob Walker. Coldness raced through Blue's arms and legs, bucked his knees, and he grabbed at Teller John.

"Get two of them gate poles, bring up a coat, a slicker if you got. We need to get him to the house.

"Thomas Ann, you go in, leave me the candle. You know what to do, girl. Hot water, find some cloths, liquor your pa got hidden. The sharp knife, soak it in whiskey. Put a flame to it. He's alive, girl. He's alive. Hurry."

Blue had seen a doctor cut into a man's chest, had had it done to him more than a year ago. And he was alive, but he didn't know about the other man. Didn't know if it could be done for Bob Walker.

There was no use asking Teller John for help; the man's face was whiter than the skin of Walker's forehead, his eyes shined an unholy light, and the big body shook in untold fears. Blue didn't bother with Teller once he read the signs.

Thomas Ann was in the cabin, mouth pulled thin, eyes flooded with tears, but her hands were steady and the condemning edge was gone from her voice. The wound demanded their attention; there was nothing to do but cut and dig, and pray: for Bob Walker, for the man who'd shot him, for the other who'd planned the raid. Blue felt the sickness come back and wished for a gulp of cold night air, a long pull at the whiskey bottle, a forgetfulness that would leave him peace.

The kerosene lantern sputtered, threw odd shadows on the

121

small cabin walls. Blue remembered now: They had moved Walker inside; it was time to work on the wound. Thomas Ann leaned over the rough-sawed table and wiped at the bared flesh of Walker's chest, soaked away the pooled blood. Blue lit a match, held the knife blade in the heat, watched the bright steel blacken. He cooled the blade with liberal bathings of whiskey, wishing again he could share its medicine.

When he touched the cleaned tip to Walker's skin the man opened his eyes, lids fluttering, pupils dilated. Smoked gray eyes that caught Blue's stare and held to it. A hand lifted slightly from the man's side, waved three fingers as if to draw Blue close. Blue leaned down to the signal, bit his lip, struggled to keep his balance when Bob Walker spoke to him in the hoarse whisper.

"Mitchell." His name was swallowed in Walker's pain, but Blue knew the sound. "Mitchell, ain't personal. You . . . drug . . . horse." There was a longer pause and the heavy lids folded back over the gray eyes. Blue waited, recognizing the strength still in the man.

"Nothing . . . against you. Me. Shot. Chance we . . . take. All of us."

Blue saw the face go slack with the effort, then he touched a curled hand to the damp forehead. A sigh released in Walker's chest that ended with a hard coughing. Bloody foam came to the mouth, a run of pain crossed the tight features.

Behind Blue, Teller John echoed the wounded man's cough and cleared his throat again, the sound of his voice in the splintered night jumping nerves in Blue and rattling Thomas Ann's pale determination.

"Blue, Miss Ann, let me operate. You help. But give me the knife. I can do it. . . . This time I know I can."

Something had been added to the pretty face of the big man. Something Blue didn't quite trust. Willingness, confidence, belief. But he gave the crude surgical knife to John and watched him turn the blade over, saw the clear eyes make a judgement as a thumb tested the cutting edge.

"This will do. Miss Ann, get me a candle, bring another

122

lantern, all you have in the house. Some of your strongest thread and several big needles. The kind you use for darning. Blue, I want you at my side, with lots of towels. Do what I tell you. And for God's sake, don't faint. This won't be pretty."

The man knew his skills. Blue wondered for a moment why Teller had asked the girl to work his scrapes and cuts after the Dutch ride across the plains, then he was too busy to think. Whatever sins Teller John was paying for, he operated on Bob Walker just as fine as a full-time doctor, and now Walker had his chance.

It became a long time. Teller would lift his head, tell Blue to wipe away the sweat collecting in his eyes, and would not look at Blue or the girl. Thomas Ann tried to speak up, but Teller went back to work and she did not dare to interrupt. The grim set to Teller's mouth, the sag to his wide back, was all the answer she really needed.

Then the brutal work was finished. Teller placed a folded pad on Walker's chest, then had Blue lift the man and hold him while a second, thicker, pad was pressed to the wide exit wound and bound in place with muslin strips. Walker breathed in short gasps as Blue lowered him onto the slab bed, and there was no color in his face but for the blue cast of his compressed mouth. Thomas Ann stroked the face with gentle fingers, and tears streamed down her own white cheeks.

Teller broke into the growing depression with startling words, "Blue, Miss Ann, he's got a chance. Which does surprise me. But his heart is regular, his pulse stronger than I would have thought possible. It is a small chance, to be sure. But it's better than no chance at all."

The same thought came to Blue and the girl at the same time, and they turned to Teller. It was as if he had been waiting for their unasked question.

"I studied medicine, briefly, in Boston. Massachusetts. There was a . . . small scandal and I left. Several years ago. Several years. But I had done surgery under supervision. It's

123

all right. I'm surprised it took you both so long to think to ask.

"Now, Miss Ann, we're going to have to deal with your father and his, ah, partner, in all this. They will not be put off by simple explanations. I am afraid I will have to remain here and tell the truth."

Blue shook his head and saw Teller's back stiffen, his head turn, eyes hard and unexpected. As if performing the operation, using himself as he had been trained, had put something back in the man, something that had been missing for a long time. Still, what Teller suggested was plain suicide.

"Teller, old son, you be waiting here when Blaisdel and his crew ride in, he sees that man shot and lying close to death, there won't be no meeting of the teachers and doctors to discuss your fate. The son of a—sorry, Miss Thomas Ann. That Blaisdel'll shoot you down and be glad of it. And no one will fault him for the deed."

Thomas Ann nodded vigorous agreement. They must leave, before Mr. Blaisdel killed Teller John. She pushed at Blue, looked up pleadingly at Teller John, and her face moved both men. Blue touched her lightly on the arm, and she leaned closer to him as he spoke. Teller John watched and said nothing.

"Don't lie to your pa about this, Thomas Ann. He'd learn the truth come time enough and it would sit hard on you. They'll ride storming into Teller's ranch and we'll be waiting. Something will come to stop this. Them night raids didn't turn out good, but we had to something. . . . You understand?"

The look of him then, the sorrow in the strange blue eyes, the long pale face shadowed with the night's work, tore into Thomas Ann and softened what kept her together. She stepped toward Blue, unmindful of Teller John, forgetful of her father's past words. It was the touch and feel of Blue Mitchell she needed now.

He came to her, hesitant at first, then drawn by what he could read in her tired eyes. They met near the heat of the burning stove. Blue put out a hand to hold her distant and

124

she pushed through its barrier, leaned into him and let her head rest on the bone of his shoulder. He could do nothing but put his arms around her for the comfort she must have.

Holding the girl, feeling the slide of flesh under his hands, the smell of hair in his face, the taste of tears as she let her mouth lie on his, these were unexpected, overwhelming. Not passion, not desire, but a deep caring, a strong urge to stand and protect what was offered.

Blue lifted his head away from Thomas Ann and saw the worn eyes of Teller John staring at him. He stiffened, ready to take insult if the man moved wrong. But Teller only smiled a thin, bitter smile and gave Blue some much needed advice.

"Mitchell, we got to go, get out of here. You're right, we can't stay here and not expect plain slaughter. Not fair to the girl. Miss, you tell your pa, because maybe he'll listen after Blaisdel finishes ranting and raving. Tell your pa I'm willing to come back, to tend Mr. Walker's injury. It must be kept clean and checked for infection. I may have to operate again if there is bleeding. Ah . . . but I will come only on guaranteed passage. I am not man enough to ride in here to certain death to treat an enemy. Even one I have done the injury to, even one whom I myself shot.

"You will have to ride out a storm, girl. But you hold to your words and keep talking to your pa. And maybe, maybe, Blaisdel will see the good sense of what you say."

The two men were half out the door when Teller stopped one last time and looked back to the young woman in the middle of the small rough cabin.

"You tell your pa to leave word at Finch's Corner. Don't need to give them an excuse to ride into my ranch ready for war. Although they most likely will. But, ah, both sides have made mistakes. It's time to clean them up."

Blue heard the horses ahead of them before he saw anything. He grabbed the lines to Teller's horse and yanked the animal sideways, forcing horse and rider into the shadow of a piñon grove. Teller stepped down, but it was Blue who grabbed the muzzles of both horses and squeezed lightly to keep them from whinnying as the tightly grouped riders passed too close.

They waited another five minutes before remounting, time enough to hear a man yell in surprise in the distance. A horse screamed, a shot was fired in blind haste, three loose broncs fled past Blue and Teller back toward the grassy plains. Away from the shooting men. Teller spooked and went for his rifle; Blue caught him, held him motionless.

"Quit, man. Still. They're chasing our night's work. Let them run a few more miles on tired stock. Maybe it'll wear out some of the anger we were going to dig up when these rannies see Bob Walker. We caused hell here tonight, and I got to pay for it somehow."

TWELVE

THE SHOUTING WOKE him from fevered dreaming. Bob Walker tried to lift his head, to find out about the noise, to know where he was. But there was no strength left in his muscles to respond to his commands. The effort of rolling his head to one side wore him out, and he closed his eyes, let himself float in the noise, let the sounds carry him away from the pain in his chest.

There were odd memories flashing in his mind; pictures stored behind his eyes that made no sense to his tired thinking. He recognized the blue eyes and long face of John's rider, he knew the woman's touch belonged to Whitlow's child. But he could not decide who had done the cutting on him. One thing he did know, it had been precise and accurate; Bob Walker had been wounded riding for a brand before.

But not like this, never this much burned, never this hard to take a shallow breath. He groaned and opened an eye, but the noise did not stop. Instead, a warm hand touched his skin, lightly stroked his forehead, and Walker could see enough to meet Thomas Ann's worried eyes. He tried a smile, to thank her for the care, but there wasn't enough energy in his frame to lift the muscles along his mouth.

Walker thought he heard the girl's voice rise above the shouting, thought she spoke harsh words to someone he could not see behind his closed eyes. But those sensations disap-

127

peared in his blurred mind, and he drifted back into a restless sleep.

"I don't care how you think you've been treated, Mr. Blaisdel. I am not a traitor. It is not your chest with a hole in it. Pa, don't tell me to be quiet. I've held my silence long enough and let you . . . men . . . run it your way. Your way. Now it's different, now there is a man here, wounded because of the two of you.

"Pa, I'm right. It ain't nothing Mr. John and Blue did, it's what you started by coming up here to something didn't belong to you and trying to take it anyway. It's wrong, and a good man may die because of—"

A wide hand clamped down over her mouth, and Thomas Ann struggled in its power. She choked on the acrid smell of the bitter skin, fought to free herself, until she saw her pa doing nothing but stand to one side and let Emmett Blaisdel handle her like she was a barnyard hen. It took the struggle from her.

"Missy, you said your piece, now shut the hell up. We got enough of a mess without you filling our heads with romantic garbage. Girl, you keep your goddamn mouth shut when I take my hand away, or it'll come back and knock some sense into you. Girl."

He pushed her away roughly, and Thomas Ann grabbed a chair to keep from falling. The chair turned and she reached out blindly, jerked back in sudden fright as her hand touched the hot surface of the cook stove. The singed fingers went into her mouth and she sucked on their bitterness.

No one in the crowded room moved, no one came to her rescue. Thomas Ann would not look at her father, would not see the shame reddening his face, or the faded eyes studying the floor. She saw past the silent men to the rough pallet where Bob Walker lay. Then she went to him, brushing past Emmett Blaisdel, worried suddenly at the bright spot of red on Walker's face, the quick whistling as he tried to breathe. She forgot about the burned fingers and her father's betrayal.

128

She had to take care of the patient; that way she would not have to hear anything said around her.

"That's right, old man, your own daughter sold you out, let those two sons into your own home. What you got to say about that? Makes no difference to me. She can nurse Walker here 'till he dies, then you two are on your way back off the mesa.

"I'll buy you out, Whitlow. Make a trade is more like it. I let you go—take your damnable child and get the hell away from this place. Going to break loose up here, and you ain't going to want that loyal girl a yours caught up in the tangle."

Blaisdel forgot the old man then, didn't bother with the flare of panic in the bleary eyes that was soon replaced by a bright hatred. Whitlow wouldn't pick up a gun and shoot a man to save anything, least of all his ungrateful bitch child.

The yelling and the tusseling with the girl had given Blaisdel some time to think. Time to calculate what the men would tolerate. Walker had been one of the best, a tough one to ride out, a friend to several of the men still waiting for a word. He'd turned strange after the rope ride in the meadow, but he'd kept to his word. All that counted in the world these men shared.

Rough-handling the girl wasn't the best thing Blaisdel had done this night. He knew that, knew it from the grim faces watching him. But he'd let her go quick enough, and with no dark bruises to show from his anger. It might be enough, or might not.

"Boys, we got a problem. That blue-eyed son shot Walker. Got to him for the ride, even though Walker said his sorry right to the man. It's a poor son can't handle no apology. Now, Walker don't look to make the day but he's still with us. And the girl's nursing him, even though she's best off the mesa. Out of the fighting that'll hit soon enough."

He hesitated, pulled at the scrub bristling his chin, and shifted weight on his booted feet. He was godawful tired, and unsure of where to go next. But he would corral and hold the impotent fury building in the riders ringing him. They were his, for the moment, and that could be all he needed to keep the grass.

"We can have us a meal. Then it starts. You, Clark, take Paco. You ride to John's after you done chowing. Tell them the girl says Walker needs the doc. Needs Teller John. Says it's trouble. We got to split that blue-eyed son from John's side. Then we'll see."

There was mumbling and some outright cursing, but Blaisdel figured since the men tugged hard on their hats, went out to put up the broncs, even brought in wood for the girl to get cooking, they must have accepted his words as good enough. He'd keep them listening, keep them hustling, and they'd take their pay and do his bidding. That's all riders like this bunch, or any man dumb enough to work for pay, was good for.

He'd have to be some careful, have to play this out so the mesa ranchers didn't go calling for the law in a hurry. Couldn't leave bodies behind, couldn't hang the two miserable sons ups to a high old pine like he wanted. Not like the old days, when it was a long gun and a hard mind that owned the land.

He came back to planning; Mitchell could disappear, no one would much miss him. A day-wage drifter, a nothing. Teller John, he would have to meet a natural ending. Cut his balls off and stick them in his mouth would fit, but this would have to be done with words, not sharp knives. In the meantime, Blue Mitchell would be caught out and slaughtered, tore up and buried deep, and no one would much care.

Blue hadn't thought much past Walker's chest wound and its suturing, until he tried to shrug out of his rusty shirt. The blood was Walker's, and its wide stains gave him a too close knowledge of the man's mortality.

When the buttons finally scratched through their holes and he could lift the fabric from his shoulders, the cloth stuck to his neck and he winced from the pull. A good yank freed the shirt, and he sat down in a sudden weakness. He dropped his head into his hands and wanted desperately to lie down and close his eyes.

The wetness running along the underside of his arm and down his ribs finally woke him to knowing something was wrong. He sat up slowly, let the fingers of his right hand do some exploring, and found that he had been shot.

Creased was more like it, at the joining of his neck and shoulder. The blood had dried to the shirt, and tearing it loose reopened an angry flood. Blue touched the blood, rolled it between his fingers, and was too tired to do anything but let it drip.

"Good lord man, you hit? What happened?"

It was Teller John. Quick to see the obvious. Blue had to raise his head, to grin at the worried face bent close to his. The man was a sometimes fool.

"Mister, this ain't but a little crease, a reminder how close we come tonight. Didn't know it was there. Teller, let it be. Ain't nothing."

The anger got away from him then, and Blue choked on the fury spilling up in him. He swiped at John's hand as it poked and probed at the small slice on his carcass. He'd had enough, goddamn it. The two long nights and endless days ached in him; he fought Teller's gentle hand and stood above the man, letting the blaze of his anger put unholy words in his mouth.

"Goddamn fools, we're both goddamn fools. Me for thinking I could make a difference, you for pulling a gun and aiming it at a man who dared shoot at you. We done nothing but wrong, Mr. John, and now a good man's paying for it."

There was more burning in Blue, but he didn't have the words for its escape. Teller left him then, quick to see the fire in the ocean eyes, quick to understand its source. Its life was mirrored in unplaced anger deep inside his own aching body. Teller went to the crude area used as a kitchen, stood for a long time to fiddle with making coffee. The sounds behind him let him know Blue had finally gone outside, come back in again, then headed straight to the pile of robes and blankets he slept on.

131

When Teller had got the pot boiling he left his busy work to check on the exhausted Blue. Blue hadn't bothered with a shirt, but lay across the pallet naked from the waist up. He knelt down by the man but didn't touch him, too familiar with the rider's quick response. The wound wasn't much, as Blue had said. A surface tearing of skin and flesh where a bullet had burned across him. But, good lord, the man had taken abuse in his short time. Teller shook his head, marveled at the punishment a man's body could suffer and survive if the man himself had the depth of heart. Teller knew he wasn't one of these men, never would be.

It was more than his deal this time. He knew that if he'd stayed a polite Boston surgeon bodies like this would rarely have come under his hand, and he never would have known the depth of the rough and ragged men who lived such deprivation. Teller rose slowly, aware of his own battered condition, his own trembling soul. Conscious of the hell that would soon break over his head. He had better be ready for its approach.

It was an act of defiance. Teller saddled the big gray gelding, slapped the silver rigging on the broad back, slipped the finely worked silver bit into the wet mouth. His hands shook when he drew up the cinch, and they fumbled and almost dropped the new black leather case when he attempted to secure it across the cantle. Teller John was afraid.

He knew Bob Walker needed him. No rider had come to the ranch yet, no posse of angry cowmen, just the long-buried instinct from his few years of training. If Walker had lived the night he would be restless now, fevered, thrashing in his crude bed, challenging Miss Thomas Ann's soothing to keep him quiet. Stitching would be loosened, packing would shift in the gaping hole, and Bob Walker could bleed to death. Teller wouldn't have that, not even if it meant his saddling to ride back to Blaisdel's cabin.

Blue Mitchell still slept. Teller had looked at him briefly before coming out to the corral. Mitchell lay on his side, legs drawn up, hands flattened between his legs. Like a child. A deadly child. Mitchell didn't stir as Teller watched him; he moaned once and rolled his head, but did not awaken. That was fine. Today the man had earned his sleep.

Teller thought a long time before he slid the rifle out of its fancy carved scabbard. This time he would go unarmed. This time it was an errand of mercy, an act of conscience. He would not need a weapon to protect himself. And then Teller laughed quietly at the noble breadth of his thoughts. He sounded like one of the thin, badly-printed paper novels about the West, novels written by a glory man scheming for a dime. Blaisdel and his men would shoot him down despite his rare sentiments, despite his going unarmed into their camp. He shoved the rifle back into the scabbard, hard, and rewrapped its ammunition in a pocket handkerchief. At least he would not carry a handgun; he was no good with one in any case.

His knees weakened, his face was damp, he licked dry lips. Teller mounted the gray and swung the horse out of the yard, reined the horse down the rutted track that passed near Blaisdel's cabin. He would have prayed, but that ability had left him before his journey west.

Two riders appeared next to a thin stand of piñon. Teller didn't know who they were, but he recognized the hands touching the pistol butts, the swing of restless horses. Blaisdel. They had to be from Blaisdel's crew. He swallowed the cry lodged in his throat and kept the gray on a steady line along the track. The riders made no move for him, let him pass them at a distance, and then they swung into line behind him. The gray tried to wait for their company; Teller slapped the horse with the knotted ends of the reins, pressured his sides with spur-less boot heels. The gray steadied and walked on; the two men behind him let their horses pick up a slow jog that brought them to almost touching the gray's quarters.

Teller would have spat the foulness in his mouth, but he would not lower his dignity to such a move. He wanted to wipe the sweat from his forehead, wanted to scratch at the itch riding his back. He sat rigid on the big gray and held the horse to the long track.

* * *

133

The rider named Clark kept his hand to the familiar butt of his pistol. He didn't figure what the rancher was doing ahead of him, he couldn't figure why the man would ride back into Blaisdel's anger. Clark didn't bother to glance at Paco; the man would know nothing, see nothing. There were no answers in Paco's mind, only orders. And their orders had been to ride to Mr. John's place, bring him out, cut him free from that blue-eyed ranny, and ride him to Mr. Blaisdel.

Clark shook his head, wondering hard on what he knew, what he saw. Here was Mr. John riding for them, packing a big black bag high to the back of his fancy saddle, riding right past them as if they didn't have pistols and crossed belts and wild eyes and bad reputations.

The man was riding for Blaisdel's quarters, which was what Mr. Blaisdel wanted. So Clark and Paco would ride along behind. Following orders. Clark laughed to himself at the feeble joke, and was aware that Paco was looking over at him, had even pulled the unlit cigarillo from his mustached mouth and opened his maw as if to ask a question. Clark grinned at the sour man and Paco shut his mouth like a sprung trap. Then they both touched spurs to their broncs; Mr. John had let the gray pick up stride and the big horse was eating up the ground.

THIRTEEN

WILLIAM FINCH ONLY half listened to his son. He knew better, he knew the boy had poison on his tongue, bile filling his throat. But still he listened.

The boy's bitter mouth had stirred up trouble before, long before the Finch family had come to the dusty mesa and claimed their small corner of the land. Only a week or so ago, lost time in William Finch's mind, his son, his blessed first child, had spoke out against Miss Annie Whitlow. It was as if the devil rode inside Jacob Finch and was loosened and released when others did not do to his liking.

The Whitlow girl had been seen riding with Teller John's man, that one named Blue Mitchell. She had tended his scrapes and bruises at Mr. John's insistence, then had ridden with the man one afternoon. Jacob had turned her innocent behavior into a scandal, one the mesa families took to their hearts.

William Finch knew of small hearts and minds, of the loathsome trouble they could cause when given a one-sided set of words that were stated as facts. In this case the facts were clear and plain, and it was his son, his first-born Jacob, who was providing the twisting, the pinched-mouth words to condemn a young girl and a hard-used drifter. William Finch would prefer to trust Blue Mitchell, to enjoy the shy innocence of Thomas Ann Whitlow and her smile, and not listen to the vile accusations of his child.

The boy rattled on, like his ma, until William Finch let the legs of his chair hit the hard dirt floor as he came forward in the caned seat.

"Boy, I've heard enough of you fussing over that girl, you ain't showed a penny's worth of thought yet. Now you're trying to tell me she's loose and whoring around with that man Mitchell.

"Boy, I ain't much fond of Mr. Whitlow for what he's doing, but he's got all the signs of a good man worried over his girl. Man's sick, that's real easy to see. And the child is all he's got for him.

"Don't you speak up while I'm talking! You've been better taught than that, boy. Now Miss Thomas Ann, she may have her own ideas, but that child knows her way, and I won't sit here and listen to you mouthing on what she's doing. It's your own base wishing you talking about, boy, not what that girl might have done. Quiet now! It's enough!"

He slammed both hands on the flat side-arms of the chair; the loud crack brought his son's head around in a violent twist. Damn the boy; too much like his ma's brother, even to the hooded light eyes and beaky nose. William tried real hard with his son, his first-born. Tried to find the love in him for his own, his only son. But he was coming to learn he did not have the charity for loving his male offspring.

The girls were a blessing: bright-haired, leggy, quick to smile at their beloved papa, quick to do their ma's bidding. Sitting with them at night, one child reading to a younger, one helping Miriam with a ball of yarn, one learning to do the quick small stitches of fine mending; all this William Finch treasured. But he did not treasure his son, his Jacob.

The boy was a ferret, a yellow-striped skunk, and it wasn't difficult to know the boy felt his pa's mind, lived with the utter lacking of love. For Jacob's washed eyes held a rare glowing light, and when he sat to hear his father's words the light grew brighter, harsher, as if the flame of hatred were fueled by the useless talk.

Finch sighed deeply, ran his left hand across the smoothness of his skull. He'd brought the family to this mesa for peace and safety; things he prized deeply above a fine store and a hard wool business suit, a bowler hat and the sound of money. Stores burned, business failed, children talked and started rumors, but the land was a constant source, an unending gift. He'd chosen this mesa with much careful thought. That the rise of the land was beautiful had never occurred to him; it was land unblessed by water, impoverished by hard base rock and dried streams.

The mesa belonged to him by its unnatural dry seasons; for cattlemen and big ranchers shunned the thin grass. The mesa was perfect for William Finch and his brooding. Even the few small ranchers already settling in the area had no edge of greed to them, no urge to hold and fight. William Finch was tired. But there were still some wrongs that must be righted, even with the hard edge of his own son.

"Jacob, you take your mouthy words off that girl. I met your Blue Mitchell, right here in the store that morning. He looked a good man; maybe rough eyes and a face would invite a fist, but he's a good one. Miss Annie will be safe as a babe with him.

"Jacob, you shut your mouth about what you think you saw to the meadow. You caused enough trouble, boy, with your hateful words. Now you shut your talking on the girl and leave it be. What you been saying ain't right, and I will no longer let a son of mine speak so. That is settled."

Jacob Finch hated his pa when he talked down to him. He hated him even more when the old man tried to tell him about Miss Annie. As if the old man could know anything. Jacob Finch hated easily, and deeply. He had had a lifetime of learning how to hate.

So he worked his daily chores, listened to the small ranchers as they rode into Finch's Corner, bought their pitiful supplies, stood and talked carefully of the doings to the mesa. Jacob listened, grinned when anyone took notice of him, and kept his thinking to himself. He would have his time, and it would be soon.

It was Aaron Fletcher who drove in two days later, full of

137

slow-spoken talk about doings on the mesa. The frail old man didn't even look at Jacob but handed him the lines to his faded, speckled gray mare and limped up the few steps to what served as the community post office.

Jacob followed the unspoken orders quickly, tied the gray mare under a shade tree, wound the frayed lines around the whip socket, and silently went up those same stairs, ducking his head and hunching his shoulders so no one in the narrow store would take notice of him. He had to listen, had to hear what brought the old rancher back to Finch's Corner so soon after his last trip. Jacob knew the tale would be something for him to use. He knew it as much as he knew anything.

His pa looked at him quickly, shook his head, and raised a hand as if to shoo Jacob away, but said nothing as he heard the old man's wild talk. Jacob leaned his back to a board, felt the soft breeze of air come through the wide slats in the poor wall, and listened to the sputtered words.

"Don't know what's happening up here, William. Don't rightly know. I tell you, that Emmett Blaisdel, he's got to wanting too much. Too much. Taking from us . . . too much.

"You hear 'bout the goings-on? Shooting, there's been. And chasing cattle. Hell's coming for us here, William Finch. Hell's coming."

Jacob looked at his pa, as if the sounds would translate on his pa's face. As if his pa could understand the fluttering words of Aaron Fletcher. But Pa had nothing on him, nothing past a cold, drawn-in look that would almost have frightened Jacob if he were still a child. Jacob looked away, stared out the door, waited patiently.

He was not disappointed; Fletcher found his breath and rattled on, coughing and wheezing through the labor.

"That-there man of Teller John's, that Blue Mitchell, he got him an idea to run Blaisdel's prime cattle. Done it two nights in a row. Teller John rode with him. Damndest thing I heard."

Fletcher had to stop, hack violently; William Finch sat motionless and made no neighborly offer of water, no gesture of help. Jacob did not move. Not even when the old man spat and barely missed his booted toes.

"Got us a shooting over there now. One of Blaisdel's men, some fellow named Bob Walker. Last night, so's I heard. Word come from the Whitlow girl. I don't know. . . . It's to shooting now. We ain't no longer safe here."

Jacob stopped listening then. Thomas Ann Whitlow, in the cabin of the enemy. A shooting. The hated name of Blue Mitchell connected to his Thomas Ann again. The hatred burned deeper in Jacob Finch, and he would explode with the fire it raged in him. Then the words of his pa brought back the sunlit day, the musky smell of the small, narrow room. Jacob listened again.

"Aaron, I won't do nothing. Let those men fight their own battles. The one you say is down, shot, is nothing but a hired killer belonging to Blaisdel. He's been to the store, he's ridden errands for his boss. And he's no one, like the rest of those killers. Blue Mitchell's in that bunch, if he got the raiding started. No better than Blaisdel's killers. No, I won't have nothing to do with those men.

"It was the girl told you, this morning? Frightened, out riding, headed nowhere, and stopped to talk? Aaron, I got no energy to deal with this. It don't matter, they ain't shooting at us. They don't want our land. Let them deal with each other, let Teller John figure out what to do."

His pa's voice dropped and Jacob barely heard the words: "Oh Lord, it can't happen here. Not again."

Jacob did not understand. There were tears in his pa's eyes, pale stains on his blanched face. Fear trembled the thin mouth, wiped the worn hands up against each other. Jacob knew then he had nothing but contempt for this man who had sired him. Nothing but righteous anger and pure hatred to drive him. So he kept his eyes away from his pa's face, kept his head bowed, his mouth pulled in silence. He listened to the end of Aaron Fletcher's words.

"That girl, she rode hard this morning and didn't much want to talk. Didn't make sense for me. It were wrong for a girl like her to be caught in a man's mistakes. Her pap . . .

well, I don't know, William, I purely don't know what will happen now. But it ain't for me to know or care. I guess.''

Jacob slid around the door, skipped the steps, didn't see the puff of dirt rise around his boots when he landed hard and walked quickly away. There were rough moments in his head, thinking on Miss Annie, his Miss Annie, tending to another wounded man. He knew there was charity in such care, and he knew enough to know it was what she must do. But he could see the eyes of Blue Mitchell, the man looking down at him, the destroying, beguiling smile on the long face.

Jacob kept his vision of Miss Annie touching that particular man, and fueled his anger into its raging fire. Thomas Ann Whitlow was due him; there was nothing could happen to the mesa to change that fact, nothing to keep their destinations from being together. Nothing but Blue Mitchell.

Then, midday, his pa gave Jacob a gift. A vague direction to ride out, take the old paint gelding, and even use the battered army saddle Pa sometimes rode. To go looking for the milch cow, strayed from the slat-fence pasture behind the barn. The little ones needed their milk, and the lamed cow could not have wandered far. Jacob could have the horse, the luxury of the old saddle. Pa spoke his words and passed Jacob by.

There was no one in the store, so Jacob took a few extra items he did not feel his pa would miss. An awkward Navy Colt, a handful of shells, and a frayed rope to lead in the cow.

FOURTEEN

THE OLD COW stood tied to a half-rotted piñon. Jacob Finch rolled over on his back and pulled a stalk of wild grass through his teeth. He sucked the stem of wild mint and savored the bitter flavor, the warmth of the sun. The memory of the girl burned on his eyes.

She was below him, sorrel horse tied to another piñon, cinch loosened, bridle hanging from the saddle horn. Thomas Ann Whitlow. Right where he knew to find her. That the cow had strayed in this direction was a sign for Jacob, a sign that he was to lie here and wait, hide in loose grass and juniper and bide his time.

Jacob folded and tore the stalk of grass, let the shredded pieces fall through his fingers. He would wait here a time longer; something would happen today. Something that held him quiet and at rest, something that would end Blue Mitchell on this mesa. Something would destroy the man who had kissed his Thomas Ann willingly, without Jacob's permission.

The old cow stirred restlessly, the paint gelding slept with lowered head. Jacob pillowed his head on his arms and watched the girl alone below him.

When Blue tried to stand from the bed he found his knees unsteady, his hands shaking. He was hungry. His belly rumbled, his head felt light and spinning. Pure hungry. Blue saw the blackened pot still waiting on the wood stove. There were stale biscuits scattered on a plate, and a leathery, half-chewed steak that would give him something to work on while he figured out the rest of the day.

He knew Teller was gone, had felt the shadow of the man standing over him, waiting a moment of time. As if Blue would awaken by pure thinking and talk to the big man. Blue had held his eyes shut, worked on slowing his breathing to stay asleep. He wasn't ready then to go back over the night. He wasn't ready for the pain on Teller's wide face. It was tough enough facing himself now, alone, coming awake in the middle of the morning.

Chewing on the tough meat let his mind wander, sipping at the cooled and bitter coffee swirled his thinking too fast. Blue had to ride. Almost anywhere, any place, would do. He thought again of leaving the mesa, shied back from the idea as if it were a defeat. But the idea was there, the teasing thought of riding down the rutted track and leaving all the complications behind him. All the bad judgments, all the poor choices.

But there was a girl in a rough slab cabin, and a big man with a cocksure grin and uneasy mind. A hard-handed cattleman too willing to take what wasn't his. Blue came back to thinking on the riding out, slapped his hand on his long thigh, and cursed himself in a too loud voice. It didn't matter; there was no one here to listen.

He finished all the rough meal he could stomach and piled up the tin plate and cup. He'd saddle and ride, check on Blaisdel's herd, follow its path and do some better figuring. He'd ride; that's what he was good for doing.

The bay gelding was smooth-gaited, the day was bright blue and shiny, the grass smelled sweet. Blue thought on rolling him a smoke, but the tobacco's heated taste would be foreign, wrong in the clean dry air. So he pulled at his hat brim, tugged at the grayed edges of his vest, and put his spurs to Becker Sorrell's eager cow pony.

The horse bolted and Blue went with him, long legs wrapped to the dark sides. Blue aimed the horse at a distant green patch and the horse ran easily, smoothly. Then the bay hit slick rock and skidded, went down on both knees, grunted with the effort. Blue tried to rein in the gelding but the bay came up in stride and fought the bit. Blue let the big horse run it out, laughing with him as they ran.

Horse and rider touched a wide belt of open grass and Blue asked the bay to belly-down and go. The bay leaped forward and the wind tore Blue's hat, watered his eyes, burned his face. Then he could feel the horse gulp for needed air, and Blue asked again for a slower stride. The bay gave in and dropped to a quick trot, then an easy walk. Blown out and sweated, the bay walked freely. Blue slapped the arched neck, felt his own heart pound with the small freedom of the run.

Now he would have his smoke. He tugged out the makings while the bay shifted around a piñon. Blue cursed the horse, refilled the paper with shredded tobacco, and rolled the lumpy cylinder. He lit it, drew a hard breath, and savored the acrid air brought into his lungs.

He looked up then and saw where he was, felt a shift in the brightness of the day, the glory of the running. He slid off the bay, ran his fingers hard down the suspect tendon. The black hair of the leg held the sun's warmth, but no signs of tenderness. Blue sat back on his heels then and faced his thoughts.

The bay gelding had brought him to the tumble of rock and the wide expanse of grassy plain where he had been dragged. Where he had found his fear torn open along with his skin and bone. Blue felt the uneasy sickness well up in him again, a sickness he thought had been buried by the action of the past few days.

He knew he had been wrong; the cattle raids were a bust. Blaisdel still owned the mesa without title. And Bob Walker was down, a man hard-shot and fighting to live. Blue rose quickly from his heels and spooked the bay, caught and soothed the horse, and then remounted. He was tired of beating himself with thinking; he was worn out with other people's problems that had become his own.

Cold sweat beaded his forehead. There was a figure seated on a rock below him, angled across the fallen ledge and broken trees. A horse was tied nearby; a chunky sorrel horse. Blue recognized the slenderness of the seated body, the special tilt to the dark head, and he raised his arm in gallant salute as the bay gelding snorted and bucked sideways down the hill.

"Miss Thomas Ann. A pleasure, a real pleasure, miss."

Something slapped at his face. Blue ducked and drew out the pistol from the old Mex saddle, looked quickly for the enemy. It was nothing more than a piñon branch rubbed across his face. Blue swallowed more than his pride, wiped at his stung cheek, and forced himself to ride straight at Miss Thomas Ann. As if he hadn't been spooked, as if nothing dumb like a stubby branch had him shooting at outlaws. If she spoke about his greenhorn action Blue would swing the bay around and ride away.

She had been too tired to sleep this morning. So, after Pa had promised to tend to Bob Walker if he woke, she had saddled the chunky gelding and ridden out. The wounded man had passed the night in broken, fevered dreams, but had opened his eyes and looked at her this morning, tried to say his thanks. She had put a hand gently to his mouth and shook her head no. He needed his strength for healing, not for unnecessary words.

Perhaps it had been wrong for her to leave Walker, but she needed clean air, a time away from Mr. Blaisdel and the rest of the silent men. The rock-strewn slide was a beautiful spot, peaceful in the bright sun, an easy place for a ride. And by chance she might find Blue Mitchell. She did not want to admit it to herself, but she wanted his arms about her, wanted the lean hardness of him, the odd comfort.

The day was a gift; calm, quiet, free-blowing and sweet. Thomas Ann drew warm air in over her wetted lips, touched her tongue to the corners of her mouth, found her hands raised to lightly touch her breast. She was alone and she wanted to be with Blue Mitchell.

Then the old sorrel whickered behind her and a big noise crashed through the brush. Thomas Ann jumped, settled herself, fanned her face. Blue Mitchell looked down at her, removed his hat with a grand and sweeping gesture. She smiled to herself, glanced back up at the long-haired rider as he came closer. She saw him twitch in the saddle, grab for his gun, settle back and wipe at his face. She knew there was blood on his fingers, and read the curse he silently mouthed to himself.

She moistened the handkerchief tucked in her sleeve, stood slowly, and walked to where Blue had stopped the bay gelding. She waited silently as he dismounted and tied the horse, then went to him, motioned for him to bend down, and wiped the dotted blood from his cheek.

"It's nothing, Blue. Only a scratch."

He knew that, and so did the girl. They both knew her actions were an excuse, a present for Blue. For herself. He held quiet, afraid to move a finger, blink an eyelid. He could smell Miss Thomas Ann; the cleanness of her homemade soap, the heat of her skin. Sunlight slanted in angles and planes on her face, touched and highlighted a brightness to her dark red hair. Blue wanted nothing more than to hold her, kiss her. He did not move.

The blood came back slowly in its dotted line. Trickled down his face, caught in the corner of his mouth. Blue focused all his feelings, all his reactions on the simple, pinprick sensation of that warm fluid touching his face. Thomas Ann stretched and wiped it away again. Neither of them spoke. There was nothing alive on the rocks other than the breathing of Thomas Ann and the bewilderment in Blue Mitchell. No one moved, nothing seemed to have a life of its own.

Thomas Ann broke first; she laid her head on Blue's chest, heard the deep thudding of his heart, and then felt his arms wrap around her. There was a safety here for her, with this odd-eyed man. She stepped closer to him, felt the length of him along her body, and let all the fear in her escape in a choking, tearing sob.

The sound broke Blue apart. He could hide passion, he

145

could bury his desires, but he could not deny a woman's crying. Blue drew her close, felt the sharp bones of her shoulders, stroked her back as if she were a frightened young mare. Thomas Ann shuddered hard, gulped in air, and choked on jagged cries. Blue murmured nonsense words, knowing she would feel the words, take some comfort from their sounds. There was nothing for the two of them except the warmth and feel of each other. Blue buried his lips in Thomas Ann's bright hair and mumbled all the thoughts racing through him, hid them in the luxury of her trust, smothered them in the slowing sounds of her deep cries.

She was the one, *she* reached out for the man. It was she who was the shameless one. But the man was to blame, for he stood there and challenged her, stood there and accepted her advances. She was young, she knew no better. It was he who must be punished. And it was for Jacob to do the punishing. It was meant that way.

His immature body reacted to the spied caresses of Thomas Ann, and Jacob Finch cried out his desire. She was betraying him, she was touching another the way she must touch only him. Jacob fed the anger; *he* must be Miss Annie's salvation, he must be the one to possess her soul. Her body.

So he must act, now. He must not think, he must not see the height of Blue Mitchell, he must not touch the wire muscle or look into the hard, shining eyes. He must do what was needed, ordained; he must bring down the blond rider and take Miss Annie for his own.

Jacob crawled back to the tired paint horse his pa had let him ride and dug out the dulled pistol Pa didn't know was missing from the stores. He knew it was simple: to raise the barrel until it sighted where he wished to fire, then pull back the trigger and hold himself steady, see his target. Jacob wiggled his path back to the rocks, where the man and the woman were still in their embrace. Lost to him, denying him his rightful pleasure, his righteous work in the salvation of Miss Annie Whitlow.

Jacob stood quickly, fired blindly, terrorized by the heavy

146

weight of the handgun, awed by the black power that exploded from it when he drew back on the trigger. The barrel flew out of his control; he grabbed the weapon, yanked at the trigger again, and heard the second explosion inside his head. His hands opened and the gun fell to the ground, skidded on slick grass, and rapped hard on a smooth rock. Ears still crackling with the unexpected anger of the drawn weapon, Jacob tried to look where he knew the man and woman had been. He was not yet frightened by what he had done.

There was something above them, something hidden in the scrub brush. Blue heard the different sounds over the girl's muted sobs. He rocked back on his heels, his arms stiffening as he tried to push the girl away, aware of a new danger to them. She would not leave his arms; his boot heel caught between two rocks and he stumbled, hit on his knees with one hand outstretched for balance. He heard the girl cry out then, as a stunning force shattered his head and tumbled him flat on the ground.

The noise came again; a loud, echoing crack, a high pitched scream far away, another cry near his head. Then a shocked howl, a sudden quiet. Blue struggled to bring his legs under him, fought to find the ends of his arms, to move his hands, to grab something, anything that would help him stand. He tasted a familiar wet, salty taste, thick, hot: his own blood. He'd been shot.

The girl. The second cracking. A bullet. Her silence. Her not answering to his hoarse calling. Blue rolled over, ignored the flashing light in his eyes, the thudding pound in his brain. The girl.

He could sit up now, and could move his hands enough to rub the thickness out of his eyes, open them to the hard sun's direction. The girl. She lay sprawled across rough rock, white arms frail and exposed. Legs undressed above her knees, white flesh, wrong angles, red streaks on one arm, on the back of her head, where the slenderness of her neck tucked

147

into her dark red hair, where the thick growth of fine hair turned a brighter, falser crimson.

Shot. Both of them. By someone shadowed on the rim of the piled rocks. Someone who had climbed on the back of a swayed paint and lumbered into the piñon-tangled brush. It didn't matter; they'd been shot. She'd been killed.

Tears blurred his eyes as Blue crawled over the splintered ground, reached out and touched the girl's white skin. Its smoothness, its passive acceptance, frightened and panicked him. He hunched closer to her, fought his terror, placed the tips of two fingers along the silky edge of her jaw and found the presence of her life. The sweet pulsing of blood through her veins, the gentle beating of her heart.

Drops of blood landed on her forehead, spread and joined the river of blood from her opened skin. Blue wiped his own face; the blood stopped dripping, but his fingers were dark stained. Thomas Ann moaned then, turned her head slightly, cried out from the effort, and her eyes opened wide.

"It's all right, girl, You're all right. It's—"

"Blue, your head, you're bleeding. What happened?"

She tried to pull her arms in, tried to sit up, and cried out sharply at the new-awakened pain. Her arm, the red streaking, the wrong angle. Broken, bent back to the wrist.

Thomas Ann cried, low, deep sobs. Blue let his fingers stroke her face, let himself set back on his heels and try to think. The left arm was broken at the wrist, and she had a scalded open bullet path across the back of her head. But her eyes focused on him, her memory was clear, her face pale but bright with her life.

"You got a broke wrist, girl. And a mighty sore head. Me, I got a new headache, nothin much that ain't been done before. We best get you to Teller John, to his medicines and his knowing. Wait here, girl. Wait while I find a splint, get the horses. You wait, it'll be better soon."

He staggered into a walk and held one hand to his head, pinching his face to ease the throbbing. A quick touch let him know the crease was drying, scabbing, would not bother him much longer. His hat lay on the ground, rolled and flattened in his fall. Blue began to bend over to pick it up, and the top of his head blossomed, exploded; the lights came back, the day disappeared. He stood still, held his head carefully, forgot about his hat.

The bay gelding had pulled loose in the shooting and was standing nose-to-tail with Thomas Ann's chunky sorrel. Blue led both horses downhill, holding to the bay's saddle as the horse picked the way. He could see the girl, half sitting, holding one arm cradled in the other. The ride would be hell for her, but Teller John would work his magic and she would rest in comfort.

He found broken branches, worn smooth with wind and rain. One was cupped to hold her palm, one was thick and wide, almost flat. They would do as splints for the bent wrist. Blue shrugged out of his shirt, winced at the echo in his head as he tore long strips of faded rose. He first used precious water from Thomas Ann's canteen to wipe her face, erase her tears, give her a sip to clear her mouth. Then gently, with indrawn breath and heart pounding in his ribs, he wiped the blood from her arm, wrapped a layer of cloth across the wound, tied the crude cradle along her wrist. Thomas Ann paled and her eyes rolled back in her head, but she bit into her lip and did not cry, did not faint.

He tied the sorrel's reins to his saddle; to hell with the slow, reluctant beast. The bay was steady; Blue would hold the girl in front of him and ride to Teller John's. She cried slightly when he lifted her into the saddle, and immediately sagged into him when he climbed in back of the old Mex rig. Her weight on his chest, her closed eyes and parted mouth gave him a catch in his breathing, a hole deep in his heart. There was a stickiness at the back of her head that leaked onto Blue's bared chest. He wanted to wipe away the smear but he was reluctant to disturb the girl.

The bay walked easily, the girl rocked in the old saddle and swayed in Blue's arms. His eyes blurred, his head swelled and pushed against bone. The sun burned across his shoulders and sweat trickled under his arms, between his flesh and the girl's matted hair. Each step of the horse, each sound in

149

the fresh day, dulled Blue's mind, tired him with trying to remain awake, alert. Then Thomas Ann mumbled mis-shapen words, garbled sounds; Blue felt the heat of her body and knew she was in fever.

The bay gelding stopped; Blue jolted forward, Thomas Ann cried out. A thin brown face peered up at the burdened horse, one of Teller John's men.

"Get the boss, get Mr. John. Hurry, you. He's needed bad."

"Señor, Mr. John ride out long time ago. He tell me noth-ing. He ride out on his fancy gray."

Blue couldn't understand the man, couldn't hear the words. Then one of the faceless men came to Blue's knee and stared at him. Blue fought for the words, spat them out of his dry mouth;

"Where's John gone to? Son of a bitch, tell me. . . ."

The sly man mumbled his words, turned away his face, and spoke into the dry yard.

"Went back to Blaisdel's place. Told us to get back to working on them springs. Guess he's gone doctoring. Took him that black bag got all his medicines. 'Bout mid-morning."

Blue heard the name, shifted on the humped back of the bay gelding, and Thomas Ann cried out in his arms. Blaisdel. He shuddered deeply, and the creased tear on his head burned, throbbed, threatened to lay him on the ground. Blaisdel.

He didn't think, but turned the bay gelding out of the yard, back down the road. It was Teller John at Blaisdel's. Blaisdel.

There was no time left to him when Blue reined in the horse at the cabin's back door. Thomas Ann was crying softly now, gentle liquid moans that bubbled through her mouth. Blue was numb; his arms deadened, his head swollen to hide all surrounding sounds. He looked at the crude door hung on leather hinges, wondered who would open it and come for the girl. Who would look out and see the enemy riding into their camp.

Hands took the girl from him; he resisted until a strong

150

voice told him it was all right to let go. Then he was empty, perched at the back of the saddle, the Navy Colt angled in the old holster carved into the Mex saddle, out of his reach. Blue knew he needed to have the feel of the old gun in his hand. Faces looked up at him, white-skinned faces with pale eyes and glowing hatred. He reached forward for the weapon but something pushed him from the side and he slid from the bay's rump. Landed hard in the dirt, looked up at booted legs, spraddled wide, fancy-stitched. Legs that multiplied until he was surrounded.

FIFTEEN

THE RIDE TO the crude cabin took too long. Teller finally hurried the gray, reached behind him, and held down the black satchel when the big horse picked up in a lope. In his mind, Teller checked and rechecked his work of last night, wondering if he'd left anything untouched, hoping none of the crude stitches gave way in the man's delirium. It wasn't until he rode in behind the cabin and hollered and a white-faced man came out with a drawn pistol, threatening him, that he remembered he had done the shooting, he had sparked the showdown.

"Wait, I've come to check on Mr. Walker. You're Goddard. Wait, ask Blaisdel."

He clutched the comfort of the black satchel and froze on the big gray. It was Buel Goddard; Teller would never forget that face from the distant day at Finch's Corner when Blue had rode the man down.

"Let me at least look at Walker. I came here to help."

There must have been something in his pleading that soothed Goddard's natural instincts, for the man sheathed the gun and turned his back on Teller without bothering to speak. Teller took this as an invitation to step down, and he tied the gray with a slip knot, considering he might have to make a hasty departure.

No one glanced up at him when he entered the hot kitchen. It was as if he did not exist, or had no powerful importance.

The patient lay on a crude pallet in a corner, and Teller could see signs of the girl's attention to the man. His face was damp-cleaned, a pan and freshly folded cloths lay nearby on a rough table. Walker's head showed above neatly folded linen, obviously changed since the rude operation of last night.

"Where's Miss Annie now?" There was no answer to his question, so Teller faced the father.

"Your daughter did a fine job here as a nurse, Mr. Whitlow. You should be most proud of her."

The old man didn't have a chance to speak before Emmett Blaisdel raised his voice.

"Without the girl we wouldn't have none of this mess. You, John, you come here as much looking for that missy as you come to clean up your work. And that ranny you hired on, he been sniffing around that girl too long. It 'pears to me you come here thinking to do your duty. Well, you owe a big debt to Walker, and a bigger one to me. Only reason I let you walk in here on both feet. Do your work, doctor. 'Fore I change my mind."

Teller bent to the chore, frightened by the tone in Blaisdel's hard words. He peeled back the clean covers and unstuck the wadded pads that served as compress bandages. The heat of Bob Walker's skin shocked him: hot and parched, as if bleached dry by the gaping wound. But the man's pulse was surprisingly strong, and there was some color in his face. Not the high red of strong fever, but a smoothed blush. He had a chance, a better chance than Teller had given him last night.

Teller cleaned around the chest hole, folded and packed new bandages, and listened to the man's drawn breathing. When the gray eyes opened and looked at him, when the man moved his mouth in the semblance of a smile, Teller was again stunned by the terrible, invulnerable toughness of these cowboys. By rights of a flattened bullet, Bob Walker should be dead or dying, yet here was the man grinning up at him. A sickbed grin more like the rictus of a death's head. But a grin.

Tom Whitlow came and stood at Teller's side.

153

"Thomas Ann, she stayed with the man most the rest of the night. Come this morning we had some words. . . . She rode out early. I don't know—"

Blaisdel broke in, as if only he had the right to speak.

"Whitlow, ain't bad enough your child sided with them men, now you're talking friendly to the killer. Leave it be.

"And you, Dr. John. You finished working on your dead man? He'll live or die never mind what you do to him. 'Cepting it was you put the bullet in him."

Blaisdel had something on his mind; Teller stood straight, heard an unpleasant sound that was becoming too familiar, and knew before he turned around that Blaisdel had a gun. Loose in his big fist, wobbling as he spoke, as if Teller weren't an opponent worth considering. The insult rubbed hard, and true. Teller's knees shook; he spread his hands wide, shifted his weight, and waited for Blaisdel's cruel words.

"John, you come right to me this time. I ain't a forgiving man. You done run my cattle and killed my men. Got eye—by God—witnesses to your violence. Got the word of them farmers to Finch's Corner that it were you started the war between us.

"So I own you, Teller John. Hold you right in my hand, like a straight flush. And my hand's got a gun tagged to it, a bullet holding your name inside. No one here'd blame me for shooting you where you stand. You're a murdering son of a bitch, Teller John. I got me my proof, lying right there behind you. That man won't last the day. Goddamn you."

Teller knew the man's words didn't ring true, that the anger was faked, acted, that Blaisdel was pulling into himself to set up for the killing. Teller watched the black line of the gun barrel circle slowly, point down at Bob Walker's chest, then lift and sight down on his own trembling body. Saw the man's knuckles whiten, saw the trigger ease back, the hammer lift and stand poised. He was crying inside, shaking so much that his teeth ached from holding to each other. But he stood still and watched his own execution.

"I got you, Teller John. And I don't aim to let go unpunished what you did. I got you."

154

A fearful cry formed in Teller's throat but did not sound. Blaisdel's hand twitched again. Old Tom Whitlow stepped sideways, away from Teller John, past Blaisdel's aim. The old man was useless; head down, eyes tracked to the floor, pale and shaking. The old man held himself still, separate from the two men set on murder.

But it wasn't time yet; Buel Goddard's white face came into focus, lean and leering, grinning the death's-head smile Teller feared. It would be a cold-blooded murder in this room, and no one would even move as it happened.

Blaisdel spoke again, as if he enjoyed the bitter sound of his voice.

"My men are out guarding the steers. From you, Teller, and your man. And the girl's riding for comfort, probably gone to the arms of her lover. Your man, Teller, your man. Like that, do you? I got more. A fresh grave, a neighbor next to it. No tombstones, no ceremony, no glory. Just cold and goddamn death. You and that Blue Mitchell rider. And my man, poor gun-shot Bob Walker. A shame, Teller. A shame."

Then a noise Teller didn't hear, a violent beating cry, sounds of pain and fear, yelling that would not stop. He thought he'd died then, thought he'd given up what little courage kept him standing in front of Blaisdel's gun instead of howling his fright to the sky.

The sound raised its fury; Whitlow shoved by Blaisdel, pushed the gun barrel from its line, hurried by with no thought to his own life or death. Teller recognized a voice. Blaisdel spun around, pure hatred flushing his face. But Buel Goddard was the first one through the doorway, weapon drawn, shoulders back and tense, eyes quick to seek out the new threat. Tom Whitlow was one step behind him.

It was the old man who took command, who spoke up and made everyone listen.

"Don't touch him. Leave him be. Goddard, no."

The voice wavered then it its fierceness, but the legs surrounding Blue stopped moving, stepped back. Blue thought to get up but there wasn't enough life in him yet. Then the voice continued and Blue listened.

"He's brought in Thomas Ann. She's hurt. He's brought in my child. My girl. You don't touch him, now. You got no right. Doc, help me. Help me."

The wrinkled face came close to Blue's, peered into his eyes, showed concern in the narrowed look, the deep worry lines. It was the old man, it was Thomas Ann's pap. Blue had to explain, had to apologize, had to make everything all right.

"Didn't shoot her. Some kid, a paint horse. Saw him . . . ride."

That put it together in Blue's numbed mind. Jacob Finch; she called him Jakey. The sly-faced kid who rode his horse between Blue and Thomas Ann. Who spouted wild words and mean thoughts, and yet Thomas Ann apologized for him. Blue braced his arms in front of him, tried to rise on his own. Saw the old man hold out a hand, and had to think before he understood what was being offered to him.

The standing was hardly worth the effort. Somewhere along in the riding his legs had come to rubber under him, his knees bent themselves backward, and he had mush for ribs to keep him upright. Blue hated himself as he leaned on the old man's shoulder and stumbled to the doorway. He hated that each step threatened to buck and throw him, like that almost forgotten bay roan outlaw.

A figure rose up in front of him and the old man let him go. A white-faced ghoul who didn't move. Blue thought wildly of the old Navy Colt still hung in the saddle, staggered blindly, and pushed himself into the white-faced man, leaning heavily on the form of Buel Goddard.

It was panic that wrapped his arms around Goddard, held the man's fist away from his holstered gun. It became a clumsy dance with two reluctant partners. Whitlow's voice came up from the ground; Blue saw the shape of the man kneeling in the dust. Kneeling near the rumpled form of his daughter. There was another, larger, steadier shape touching the girl, nodding a big head, running expert fingers along the crude splint Blue remembered fashioning.

It was Whitlow's wavering voice that interrupted the bear hug, and Blue welcomed the distorted sounds.

"Goddard, you ain't been listening to me. This man walks free. I pay part of your wages, boy, so you listen, you son of a bitch. You take heed and do what I says. Let the man go."

Sharp sounds drowned out the old man. Goddard stiffened and shoved Blue hard from him. Blue went to one knee, dropped his head, swallowed hard at the rush of fluid in his mouth. Fought the dizzying circles in his head. Red lines trickled past his opened eye, and he had the time to watch two droplets land gently on the dusty ground. Words swirled around him, angry buzzing sounds laced with authority. But no one shot at him, no one knocked him over, when a crawling babe could have laid him out. No one seemed to care anymore, and Blue was comforted by being left alone. It was quiet for a long time, then a laced and veined hand came down and demanded his attention.

It was the old man who guided Blue inside, pushed him gently into the hardness of a straight-backed chair. Blue didn't much care. The simple act of walking had brought back the pounding in his ears; nothing made sense, nothing figured out to him in a way he could understand. People moved and crossed in a heated kitchen. He could see out a rough-sawed window into a large meadow. It was pretty sitting here.

He dropped his head into his hands and let all sound, all thought, leave him. Except for the knowing that Thomas Ann was being cared for, except for seeing the big shape of Teller John by her bed. It had to be enough. Emmett Blaisdel would soon demand payment in full. Footsteps echoed inside his brain, and Blue gave himself the luxury of nodding off into a clean, unconscious sleep.

It became dark outside, and Blue knew he was working up a hunger. A good sign: a man lived if he wanted to eat. It were nothing more than a bump on the head, nothing to keep him from eating something, anything, and soon if he could manage.

He straightened slowly in the chair, aware now of more than the hunger in his belly. People moving in the room, small noises, whispered words. He rubbed his hands along his thighs, saw small prints of stained blood on the pale denim, and began to remember. The terror of the afternoon's ride, the awful consequence of the embrace in the silent grass. His head ached; he groaned and tried to raise his eyes.

His voice almost worked, but the first words were rusted in his throat.

"How's the girl? Thomas Ann. She all right, Teller? Looked broke to me, her wrist. Her head, that wound on the back . . . ?"

It was the old man who came to him, stood next to him. The old voice was low and insistent.

"Boy, keep still. My girl, she's fine. Don't want Emmett thinking on the why of you being here. She's got a broke wrist and that crease back of her head. Doc says nothing permanent of the wounds. What got into the Finch boy, shooting at you and the girl like he did, I don't know. Thomas Ann's going to be fine, just fine. And I thank you for bringing her in that way. Thank you much. But you keep still now, boy. Emmett, he's pure angry you being here. Pure angry at everything, this time."

Then hell came at Blue in the shape and form of a loud man with a big voice and a bitter smile.

"Mitchell, get up. I call you out, boy. Buel, give the man your gun. No one son of a bitch robs me the way you've done, Mitchell, then rides into my place and figures to be left alone.

"Mitchell, you stand to fight. Or take your death setting there. Don't much matter to me. Both ways, you're dead."

Blue sorted through the threats, raised his head, saw the room swell and recede in front of him. A gun came into his line of sight, a fine blued Colt with dark grained grips. The fist wrapped around the offering was pale and dusted, the fingers tapered, the palm soft and uncallused. It was Buel

Goddard's fist, Buel Goddard's gun. And it filled Blue's hand easily, slid into his loose grasp like it was home. Its weight was a comfort, and Blue was able to look up at Emmett Blaisdel, take the measure of the man who would kill him this time.

Emmett Blaisdel had taken enough: first his fat cattle scattered and hightailed around the mesa, then a good hand shot in his own backyard. Now a puny girl lay on a pallet in the corner, face bound in clean bandages, arm wrapped in hard casing. The men supposed to be out herding steers had come in silently, faces long and sad, eyes questioning. As if the girl paid their wages. These men were mooning over her. As if she were a lover to them all.

It all came back to the odd-eyed bastard who sat in the hard-backed chair, head rested on the wall, long jaw and pale throat thrown back, blond hair twisted around his face. It all came back to the light in his damned eyes, the hard grin plastered on his face. Emmett Blaisdel had had enough of this one.

Mitchell rose slowly to the challenge. Blaisdel grinned at Buel Goddard, sharing a ready-made joke with his foreman. Then Mitchell lifted Goddard's Colt hanging in his fist, his fingers bent around the grip, the trigger left untouched. Blaisdel readied himself, but knew the man would not cold-fire. He kept his own hand close to his weapon but watched the rider's fist as it moved around the room.

The gun barrel drew a circle through the cabin; Blaisdel eased his own fingers, let them splay across the cold metal of his Colt. Mitchell swayed gently, shoulders supported by the wall. Blaisdel wondered if this was a trick; the blue barrel had found a target by resting on his chest. Blaisdel gripped his weapon, looked hard at the man. But there was no building fury in Mitchell's eyes, no killing light. The man was weak-kneed and wandering in his head. Blaisdel relaxed, stroked the oiled leather holster, let his head nod once to Goddard's unspoken question.

Teller John and the girl's pap were bent over the narrow

pallet, talking close in low whispers, unaware of what Blaisdel had set in motion.

"Take it outside. No shooting here. Take it . . ."

The voice was weak, barely enough to hear. Bob Walker's voice. The man had struggled to sit half against the wall. He spoke directly to Mitchell, as if Blaisdel and Goddard weren't in the room. As if Blaisdel didn't pay him his wage.

"Knew it would get to this. . . . Both of us. Girl you brought in, sleeping now." The man took a deep breath and coughed; Blaisdel thought it was the end of him, but Walker found another breath. Mitchell had stepped away from the wall, closer to Walker's bed. The man swayed and turned, but stayed erect on his wide-spread legs. The Colt in his hand was almost forgotten.

"Blue, outside. Ain't fitting . . . her to see a man die . . . lie down with the dead."

Blaisdel didn't understand but Mitchell did, for something passed over his face and Blaisdel felt cold fear. Saw the true measure of the man as he walked inches from Blaisdel without seeing him, turned his back to Blaisdel as if the promise to kill meant nothing now. When the rider came close to him Blaisdel could see the depths of the blue-green eyes, the strong pain holding the wide mouth, the effort to walk. He glanced away, saw his own hand tightened to white knuckles on the carved ivory handles of his pistol. And knew for a moment he was afraid.

Then Mitchell was past him, staggering toward the low doorway, and Blaisdel was no longer lost. He saw the crusted brown stain on Mitchell's skull, heard the shuffling steps, could not see the bright blue eyes. There was nothing dangerous in this man now, nothing Blaisdel couldn't handle. With Buel Goddard as his backup, there weren't nothing the two of them couldn't bring down.

The air held thick around him, molasses-strong, grabbing his arms and legs in a warm, slow grip. The pistol weighed an unfamiliar bulk in his fist, the angles of his knees and legs went wrong, his head shifted and blossomed in sickening

160

degrees. But still he could hear Walker's voice, could understand the man's words. That the girl must not witness what was to happen.

Blue almost could see Walker's face; he nodded his understanding, turned away, and could see a blur of faces, a bulk of a man he passed too close. But it was getting to the outside that held him erect, that kept him going. Blue bent over and passed through the low door, lost his balance from the thumping inside his brain, hurried to catch up with himself. He wasn't certain of why, but he knew Blaisdel would follow him. And Buel Goddard.

He waited in the dark. Footsteps caught his attention. Blue swung around, spread his feet wide, thumbed back the strange pistol's hammer. It was pure night, black with dimmed starlight. A shadow went to Blue's left, a bigger shadow faced him. A voice came out of the darkness that Blue struggled to understand.

"Mitchell. Get ready."

It was enough; Blue saw the vague hand lift a pistol; he raised the weight of his own gun, still foreign to his hand. Something moved on his left. He should fire to that shape first. His mind knew it was the more terrible danger. But the shape in front of him laughed a bright, teasing chuckle, and Blue pointed the gun as if it were his finger, felt the hammer slip. The air split with exploded sound and Blue knew he must draw back the hammer, swing to his left, and fire again.

The shadow's gun flashed its fire. Nothing pounded into Blue. He turned away, lifted the Colt, heard the hard click of the hammer. Then the big shape must have fired again, for the night roared and Blue felt a burning air cross his face. Instinct swung him around and he fired without thought. A harsh grunt came with the sound, the shape before him folding in the middle.

"Goddard, stop. It's done. Blaisdel's down."

A familiar voice, an old man's voice. Blue turned to its comforting sound, barely aware that the shadow to his left had crouched down, still held a gun.

"Goddard, don't."

Buel Goddard fired with the rightness of knowing he avenged the boss's death. He savored the bright flare of his second gun, the splitting noise, the angle of the man he hit. Mitchell was down on his knees, praying to the pine-scented ground. Buel Goddard rose above him, raised his pistol one more time, and laid its hot barrel against Mitchell's pale hair. The man did not move, did not know. Goddard could see the long, dark stream trace down Mitchell's leg. He knew the next shot would be the killing blow.

It felt good, it was right. Blaisdel lay motionless, face-down in the sudden glare of light from the open cabin door. It was right. It was the final killing, to Blaisdel's order.

"Goddard. No."

He had to listen this time. Buel raised his head and saw the old man, standing to one side of the door. There was a rifle braced to the old man's hip, the one hand wrapped hard to the trigger. There was a waver still in the old man's voice, and Buel Goddard knew he did not have to listen.

"Goddard. No more killing."

Goddard thumbed back the hammer, and the world exploded inside him. He dropped beside his boss and his intended victim with no further sound. The night air echoed and rang with the rifle's spent power. Then the brutal singing quieted, replaced by one man's groan, raised voices, and worried calls from inside the rough-built cabin.

SIXTEEN

BLUE WOKE SLOWLY, in pained stages, until he thought seriously on going back into the deep sleep that had claimed him. He let his eyes open, let his head move gently on the soft pillowed blankets, and began to think he could stay awake this time.

Teller John sat in the corner, back to Blue, bent over the wide table he sometimes used as a desk. The man was writing furiously, wiping at a blindness in his eyes then scribbling more on the unseen paper laid in front of him. Blue could hear the sharp rustle of the quill pen, the squeak of the coarse paper.

There was a question Blue needed to ask, a question more pressing to him than the urge to relieve himself. He thought the words, heard them in his mind, but there was no sound from his mouth. He rolled his head then, and expected a flare of the pain that had been with him. There was nothing but weakness, and silence.

He had almost got his head off the pillow when the effort was too much and he drifted back into the welcomed sleep. There would be another time to ask the question; there would be another day.

He woke this time to Teller John standing over him. The man's face was shadowed by unshaven stubble, but his eyes held the familiar glint of high humor. Blue knew then that he did not need to ask his question. He grinned at Teller, rolled his head across the blankets, and had almost got his mouth open before he was asleep again.

This time he sat up without thinking, and Teller handed him a plate of beans and bread torn into pieces. He was hungry and wolfed the meal, drank a cup of Teller's bitter coffee, found it tasted good. He must be mending, to enjoy the crude meal.

"She's doing fine, Blue. That crease on her head was more bloody than serious, and the wrist is healing at a good rate. She's a strong girl, and her pa's taking good care of her. Mrs. Finch's been over there, and the Finch girl.

"The Finch boy disappeared. Rode off on that mangy paint of his, and no one up here seems to want to go find him. Hell of a mess, Blue. But the girl is doing fine. No problems there at all."

Blue thought over the litany and found several holes in Teller's speech. He knew the girl had been hurt, but he didn't know how. Couldn't see why Teller would think he cared about the Finch boy. The questions forming in his mind must have shown to Teller, for the big man settled back in his chair, hitched up his drooping pants, and began his favorite occupation.

"I wondered how much you would remember. You had a long groove taken out of your skull. The boy did that to you, along with shooting at the girl. And Goddard's shot burned a hellhole in you, nicked an artery, and let out a lot of fluid before we got it stopped up. Mind you, old Whitlow saved you that night. I know you don't remember. Believe me, the old man was your hero.

"You got Blaisdel, Blue. Shot at him once and missed, then he went point-blank at you and missed. I always read in those penny novels about fancy shootouts, with gunfighters going up against each other and killing with one quick shot. That night sure wouldn't go in a story, my friend. You two shot at each other, outside and in the dark, I'll give you. But you both missed.

"Whitlow warned Goddard, pleaded with him, but the

164

man wouldn't listen. Thought too much of his own reputation, and never believed an old man like Whitlow would stand up to him. Yessir, Goddard's shot emptied you out, and then Whitlow let that old rifle blast away and Goddard went down like a poled bull.''

The cheerful look to Teller's face disappeared, and Blue forced himself to pay more attention to the next words. Teller wiped a big hand across his features and tried to draw a smile on them. He didn't make it, and when he saw the expectant look from the wounded Blue Mitchell he let go of the pretense and came to talk on the serious matter.

"It was a hell of a night, Blue. I . . . I've never been so emptied. From base fear. And then that crippled old man up and fired away, took care of the immediate problem. He came back inside the cabin, put up the rifle, and told me I was needed outside. It was all I could do to take those steps. He told me you were alive, but he didn't think I needed to bother with Blaisdel, or Buel Goddard. And he was right.

"I was scared to my everlasting and dying days.''

Blue knew he was missing pieces of that night. He thought hard on what Teller explained, tried to put some order to the blurred shapes and wild noise. Then it came to him, slowly, and he looked up at Teller, trying to say the right thing to the shaky man looming over him.

"You must of rode into Blaisdel's camp alone. You knew the man wanted you dead and yet it was your duty to take care of Walker. No matter, no counting how you shake inside, Teller, that's pure courage. Knowing what was coming, going there anyway. That's cold fire.

"Thinking's hell on a man, Teller. Twists him harder than anything else he does. You got pure guts, Teller, riding into Blaisdel's gun camp.''

He had to lie back then, in the softness of the plumped blankets. Aware of a throbbing in his body and an utter weakness in his mind. Fear chased him too, and thinking, until he didn't know which way to head. Blue closed his eyes, let his clenched fists open, and almost heard his first soft snore.

* * *

165

Four days passed before Blue made it out of bed on his own. He kept count of the time by watching the sunrise, then waiting for the stars to line up in the night sky outside the crude window above his bed. Something had changed in Teller John, for he had a quickening to his walk, an easy swing to his arms. Blue wasn't sure of the why, but he felt better each day watching the man.

Then he tried his own steps, found he could make good time with the fine gold-headed cane Teller offered him. His leg was a bother, swollen thick below the hip with its tight wrapping of bandages, but Teller warned him to go easy, that the artery had been closed but still could open.

"Bleed you dry in a half-hour wait, my friend. Bleed you dry like a fresh-hung buck with a slit throat. Be tough eating, even if we roasted you a long time. So you be careful."

Tom Whitlow drove over in a wire-rigged cart, the chunky sorrel wrapped in broken harness. The girl rode with him, pale-faced and drawn, but as Teller helped her up the crude stairs to sit on the wide veranda there was a brightness to her eyes and a pleasure in her step.

Blue heard the commotion and made his slow way out to the gathering. Thomas Ann looked up at his approach, then suddenly found something very important in the white-wrapped arm in her lap. Blue leaned on the cane and watched her, unaware of the two men who kept their unaccustomed silence and waited him out.

She was beautiful, Thomas Ann Whitlow. With a special air to her smile, a special grace to her fine features and dark red hair. A special girl becoming a good woman. The scene on the grassy plain came back to Blue in full force then; it was the sight of Thomas Ann, the remembrance of her small hands resting on his arms, the taste of her hair drawn through his lips, the feel of her leaning into him.

He felt the blow of the wild shot above him, he saw Thomas Ann sprawled out in the waving grass, he felt the terrible clumsiness of his attempts to ease her pain.

It swept over him, and he jerked from the memory. Teller

John stood up quickly, bringing Blue back to the stilled veranda and the three people watching him.

"It's nothing, just got me a stitch. I got to move around some, loosen up these muscles been doing nothing too long. Don't pay me no attention. Mr. Whitlow, I thank you for saving my hide. And Miss Thomas Ann, it's good to see you coming around well. I got to move some, walk out this cramp."

He cursed the hobbling gait that slowed him down the steps and out into the yard. The stares from the folks sitting on the crude pine chairs felt like they would burn a hole through his flesh. Blue tried to hurry, caught the tip of the cane, staggered, righted himself, and had to stop and catch his breath. Let the new pain of his leg settle back some. He ignored the quick call from the porch and finally was able to make his way around the back of the still unfinished barn.

Sometimes he wished he had the words in him that would bring out the itch and give it a proper name. In that flash of memory on the veranda, he had tasted again the sweeping fear left from the rope ride across the plain. He'd thought it gone, hoped it'd gone with the simple act of riding back there with Miss Thomas Ann.

The girl, she was balled up in that flashed remembering. And what he could take out of his picturing was her gentleness, the taste and feel of her. Blue jabbed the spiked end of the cane repeatedly in the ground. Digging a hole, like the one he was digging for himself with his thinking.

It was for him to do, not to sit and think, not to settle in one place and grow a family and a life. Hell, he weren't growed yet himself, not enough of a man to touch his own strength, rope his own fear.

But he would face going back to the veranda and saying his piece to the girl and her pa, thanking them and Teller John. Letting them know his plans to ride on.

The trip back to the raw house was easier, quicker. Blue had traveling back in his mind; a few more days resting, some work on the bay gelding, riding out the seal brown a few times to settle the kinks, and then he would be ready.

There'd been a town back a ways. . . . Hell, there were lots of towns.

"Blue?" Her voice was sweet music. Blue halted his awkward traveling and looked at the girl who came down the steps to meet up with him.

"Blue, I . . . Let's walk a bit, give your leg more exercise. I have some things I want to talk with you. Tell you about."

This was all done with the blessings of the old man, for he looked down at Blue and the girl and nodded his approval. Blue knew a quick uneasiness in him, as if things were coming to him he didn't much want. But her voice was soothing, and he let himself walk a ways with her.

"Pa said I could tell you. He's coming to work for Teller, for Mr. John. Pa . . . well, he tries to hide it, but I know he ain't well. It's why he got in with Mr. Blaisdel."

Quick chases of fear and anger crossed her face, and Blue almost took her hand, squeezed it to give her comfort, but Thomas Ann steadied herself and let none of the distress settle in her voice.

"Mr. John knows Pa hasn't got much time. He told me when he came over yesterday to see how my arm was doing. Mr. John, he's real concerned about Pa and me. And is asking Pa to teach him all he can about the ranch, the land, and the cattle he should be grazing up here. Pa's real pleased. And so am I.

"Blue, I've been talking a lot with Bob Walker. He's doing real well now, and Mr. John says he'll be up and working soon. Going to stay on up here, work for Mr. John, sort of take over when Pa . . . when Pa, he can no longer work."

They were almost at the corral. Blue stopped, leaned on the high fence, and looked hard at the girl who stood motionless beside him, who was struggling to hold her gaze steady on him.

She was different, softer, blushing a fine color in her cheeks. And all she'd done was mention Bob Walker's name. It came easily to Blue then, that he had no need to apologize to Thomas Ann for his riding out. Or to the pa for promises not made or kept. He knew Teller would have to find a different woman to ride in the fancy courting buggy, behind the high-stepping team of matched blacks. He put a finger gently on the fullness of her lower lip and she raised her head to his touch. There was a shyness in her that pleased Blue.

"Miss Thomas Ann, I think you and your pa, and Bob Walker, you got things all nice set between you. That Bob Walker, he's a lucky man to be working with your pa and Teller John. A real lucky man."

She smiled at him, reached up and chastely kissed the side of his cheek, and Blue blushed bright red. In the corral behind them the lop-eared, flighty bay mare kicked out with an unexpected burst of energy, spooked herself with the slap of her own long tail, and circled the pen at a run. She came to a dusty, sliding halt and whinnied shrilly.

Blue laughed, and Thomas Ann laughed with him. The bay mare turned to them and whickered in the clear mesa air.

William A. Luckey was born in Providence, Rhode Island, but later went West to work with horses. "I've spent the past forty years dealing with rogue horses using my own methods to retrain and make them useful—I've evented, shown dressage, fox-hunted for twenty seasons, worked cattle, gone on five-day trail rides. I've owned over 150 horses personally, going back to when I was seven. I've actually been riding now for almost sixty years, and have taught riding for over forty years." *High Line Rider* appeared in 1985, the first of twelve Western novels published to date. William A. Luckey's most recent works are *The English Horses* (2007), and its sequel, *Burn English* (2008). Tense suspense and human drama characterize all of the Luckey Western stories and have constantly pleased readers worldwide.